Dear Reader,

What could be more romantic than a wedding? Picture the bride in an exquisite gown, with flowers cascading from the glorious bouquet in her hand. Imagine the handsome groom in a finely tailored tuxedo, his eyes sparkling with happiness and love. Hear them promise "to have and to hold" each other forever. . . . This is the perfect ending to a courtship, the blessed ritual we cherish in our hearts. And now, in honor of the tradition of June brides, we present a month's line-up of six LOVESWEPTs with beautiful brides and gorgeous grooms on the covers.

Don't miss any of our brides and grooms this month:

#552 HER VERY OWN BUTLER
by Helen Mittermeyer
#553 ALL THE WAY by Gail Douglas
#554 WHERE THERE'S A WILL . . .
by Victoria Leigh
#555 DESERT ROSE by Laura Taylor
#556 RASCAL by Charlotte Hughes
#557 ONLY YOU by Bonnie Pega

There's no better way to celebrate the joy of weddings than with all six LOVESWEPTs, each one a fabulous love story written by only the best in the genre!

With best wishes,

Nita Taublib
Associate Publisher/LOVESWEPT

WHAT ARE *LOVESWEPT* ROMANCES?

They are stories of true romance and touching emotion. We believe those two very important ingredients are constants in our highly sensual and very believable stories in the *LOVESWEPT* line. Our goal is to give you, the reader, stories of consistently high quality that may sometimes make you laugh, sometimes make you cry, but are always fresh and creative and contain many delightful surprises within their pages.

Most romance fans read an enormous number of books. Those they truly love, they keep. Others may be traded with friends and soon forgotten. We hope that each *LOVESWEPT* romance will be a treasure—a "keeper." We will always try to publish

LOVE STORIES YOU'LL NEVER FORGET
BY AUTHORS YOU'LL ALWAYS REMEMBER

The Editors

Bonnie Pega

Only You

BANTAM BOOKS
NEW YORK · TORONTO · LONDON · SYDNEY · AUCKLAND

ONLY YOU

A Bantam Book / July 1992

ISBN 0-553-44258-9

Published simultaneously in the United States and Canada

Bantam Books are published by Bantam Books, a division of Bantam Doubleday Dell Publishing Group, Inc. Its trademark, consisting of the words "Bantam Books" and the portrayal of a rooster, is Registered in U.S. Patent and Trademark Office and in other countries. Marca Registrada. Bantam Books, 666 Fifth Avenue, New York, New York 10103.

PRINTED IN THE UNITED STATES OF AMERICA

OPM 0 9 8 7 6 5 4 3 2 1

Thanks to Carolyn, Chris, Cynthia, Janet, and Lydia for their support, and to Leanne for the pennies in my jar

Love to Christopher and Scott

And to my husband Bill—happy birthday

One

"Love, Inc.? What on earth is Love, Inc.?"

Maximillian Shore pressed his intercom button as he stared at the note in his hand. "Patsy, would you come in here a minute, please?"

The very second Patsy poked her head in the doorway, he waved the note in the air. "What is this note you left me? Love, Incorporated?"

"I don't know, boss. I just took the message. I didn't interrogate her." Max reflected that as secretaries went, Patsy was a little insolent. However, as sisters went, she was okay. The relationship was easy to spot in their identical brown hair and blue eyes.

"Her?" Max asked.

"Her. I didn't catch her name, but she did say she needed to speak with you right away on a matter of some urgency."

"And she didn't mention what the urgent matter was?"

"Nope." Patsy flashed a teasing grin. "What's the matter, bro? Got an outstanding bill at our local massage parlor?"

"Sure," Max snapped back. "I spend all my evenings there." He leaned back in his chair, eyes narrowed. "What makes you think it's a massage parlor anyway?"

"With a name like Love, Incorporated? C'mon. What else could it be?" Patsy gave a saucy smile and went back out to the front desk.

What else indeed? Max wondered as he picked up the phone and dialed the number on the note.

The female voice that answered was soft and low and made Max think of candlelight, whispered conversations, and satin sheets. "Hello. You have reached Love, Incorporated. No one is in right now, but if you will leave your name and number, I'll get back to you as soon as possible. Thank you."

It made sense to have an answering machine, Max decided. That way, she could weed out undesirables—like vice cops—before having to talk with them. In some lines of business, one couldn't be too careful. Max didn't leave a message though. If she wanted to talk to him that much, she could call him back. He resisted redialing the number just so he could hear that voice again.

Max glanced at the gold watch on his tanned wrist and stood. Damn, he had promised Jackie he'd meet her at six and it was five after already. She'd have his head for being late. Well, why not? he thought ruefully. She already had everything else. The house, the car, the bank accounts. The shirt off his back.

As he shrugged on his jacket, he looked at the note again and muttered, "Love, Incorporated. Interesting name, that." It would be even more interesting to find out what a massage parlor, or whatever it was, wanted with Shore Efficiency Consultants.

Caitlin Alexandra Love couldn't wait to change clothes. She hated dresses and hose and high heels—especially high heels. She kicked them off, giving a delicate snort. They were certainly not designed for comfort and were more like ancient instruments of torture even though they did make legs look better and women taller.

Caitlin knew she was small, topping out at five feet three if she stood on her tiptoes, and possibly, hitting one hundred and five pounds after a heavy meal if she wore her winter coat. However, she didn't care. She had never cared about being bigger.

Except once, she admitted to herself. Only once in her life had she found her small stature to be a disadvantage. She hadn't been able to fight long enough or hard enough to—

Abruptly she switched her thoughts from that disturbing line and tugged on comfortable faded jeans and an equally faded loose red T-shirt.

Sighing, Caitlin stooped to pick up the discarded heels and tossed them into the closet. Her feet would never be the same, she mused as she wiggled her aching toes. She hadn't worn heels in over a year. She wore flats or sneakers everywhere, even to Sunday school. How she hated dressing up—especially to impress IRS auditors. It had worked though. She hadn't had to pay more than a few hundred dollars. Of course, it could have been her poor, baggy-eyed accountant who saved the day.

"Mom? Oh, Mom!"

Caitlin opened her bedroom door. "In here, Jordie." She heard pounding footsteps that sounded like a herd of stampeding buffalo and braced herself.

A miniature golden-haired whirlwind attacked her with an exuberant embrace. "Mom, Mom, guess what? We played Mrs. Scott's class at recess in kickball and guess what? We won. I kicked the winning ball and Mrs. Joseph said I was a good player and . . ."

Caitlin looked down affectionately at the small boy who chattered away. She ran a hand over his curly hair, so like her own. The gold-flecked brown eyes were hers, as were the upturned nose and determined jaw. There was nothing of his father in him, thank God.

"That's terrific, Jordie!" Caitlin gave him a quick hug. "I'm glad you had such a good time today. Now, do you have any homework?"

He grimaced. "Do I have to do it now? Can't I play first?"

"We're going out to dinner tonight, remember? You need to do your homework now. I have to go to work for a while this afternoon to make some calls. You can do your homework there, if you like."

"Aw, Mom, it's your day off. How come you gotta go in on your day off?"

Caitlin dropped a kiss on his forehead. "Sorry, pal. When you're the boss, sometimes you just 'gotta.'" When he still didn't look too happy, she resorted to bribery. "How about some carob granola bars when we get there? I made some just this morning."

At his sudden smile, she smiled back. They had played this scene so many times since school started that it had become routine by now. She bundled Jordie into her ancient van and headed to work.

What in the world was he doing here? Max wondered as he maneuvered his car down the narrow streets lined with warehouses on either side. Silverdale wasn't as big as nearby Charlottesville or Fredericksburg, but it was large enough to have an industrial district. And Love, Inc., sat right smack in the middle of it.

Max pulled into a parking lot much in need of repair. The only other vehicle in it was an old battered van with a bumper sticker that said LET US PUT A LITTLE LOVE IN YOUR LIFE. This had to be the place. He'd found the address in the telephone directory the previous night and hadn't been able to resist driving by to see what kind of business it was. So far, he couldn't tell.

The building was a strange one—a long, low warehouse with arching roofs. Not a very impressive exterior, but perhaps one didn't need an impressive exterior when one ran a—a what? A massage parlor? An "escort" service? He just couldn't figure out why it needed so much room. The building encompassed what amounted to a full city block, if not more.

Max parked his car a respectable distance from the dilapidated van. After all, there had to be some reason for all its dents and scratches. No sooner had he shut and locked his car door than a small boy appeared.

"Wow, nice car, mister. Is that a real phone in there?" he asked, pressing a chocolate-smeared face against the window and peering inside.

Max winced. "Yes, it is. Here." Max held out a clean handkerchief to the boy.

"Oh, no, I can't take this," the child said immediately. "My mom says I can't take anything from somebody 'less I know 'em."

"Well, your mother sounds very wise. How about if I introduce myself? I'm Max Shore."

"I'm Jordan." He offered a grubby hand.

Max shook it gravely and said, "Well, Jordan, now that we know each other, maybe you'd like to use my handkerchief to wipe the chocolate from your hands and face." Max rubbed a smudge from his own hand before giving the cloth to the boy.

"Sure, 'cept it's not chocolate. It's carob."

"Carob. Okay. Does your mother work here?" Max asked.

"Yeah. I mean, yes, sir," Jordan said, handing the dirtied handkerchief back to Max. "She's makin' phone calls and stuff today."

"Phone calls?" Did that woman dare make God only knows what kind of phone calls while her child wandered around the streets?

"Jordie! Get back in here right now, you scamp. You know you're not supposed to play out there."

She was an angel, Max thought as he looked up, complete with golden curls and dimples. Well, he amended as his eyes swept over lush curves, maybe not quite an angel. After all, that was *the* voice. The voice that had haunted his dreams the previous night. A voice guaranteed to make a man long to hear it husky with passion. A voice that ran a massage parlor? Or an escort service? Or a sex-by-phone racket? And what did that *voice* want with Shore Efficiency Consultants?

No time like the present to find out, Max decided, walking over to her and holding out his hand. "Hello, I'm Maximillian Shore from Shore Efficiency Consultants. Max."

Her eyes were the most delicious shade of brown, with gold flecks like sunlight reflecting from a pool of coffee. Her nose tilted the slightest bit at the end and her chin, though determined, was delicate and pointed. Her body was slim but all nicely rounded curves that were evident even underneath frayed jeans and a baggy T-shirt. She was what his grandfather would have called a "pocket Venus." She was what Max called pure temptation.

Caitlin looked from Jordan to a large, tanned hand with reddish-gold hairs glinting on the back of it, and well-manicured fingernails. She glanced at her hand—dainty compared with his—then noticed the dark soil that ringed every fingernail. She quickly placed her dirty hands behind her back like a schoolboy expecting a whack on the palm with a ruler.

Looking up to say hello, Caitlin had to tilt her head back to see his face. He must have been ten or eleven inches taller than she. And all of that six feet plus was lean and dangerously male. He carried himself with the kind of sheer power and easy confidence that would attract women. But not her, Caitlin told herself.

He did give her a funny feeling in the pit of her stomach though. It made her wary and she found herself inching back a little.

"Mom." Jordan tugged on her T-shirt. "Mom."

Caitlin turned to her young son. "Yes, Jordie?" Why did she feel as if she had a mouthful of sawdust?

"Mom, he has a phone in his car and everything. It's real neat."

"I'm sure it is, honey." Caitlin looked back up at Max and smiled a little nervously. "Mr. Shore, you didn't need to drive all the way over here. You could have just called."

Not on your life, Max thought. *I wouldn't have missed seeing you for anything.* "I was already on this side of town and figured I'd stop by and see just what Shore Efficiency Consultants can do for your, er, business. How would you like my company to help you?"

"Well, it was my accountant's idea," Caitlin admitted. "He wasn't very happy when I had a little trouble finding all my records for the IRS."

"I see. You're the owner?"

"I am. Caitlin Alexandra Love. I think you've already met my son, Jordan."

Her last name was Love. So that explained the *Love,* Incorporated. "What sort of business do you own?" Max couldn't wait any longer. He just had to know what she did for a living.

"I deal in organically grown herbs. Some I grow here, others I import."

"Herbs? Like for cooking?" Max tried not to show his relief that she wasn't involved in some illicit racket.

"We do handle culinary herbs. However, we also deal in medicinal herbs." Caitlin could see the skeptical look on his face and knew what he was thinking. Any mention of medicinal herbs always conjured up images of wizened old women living in one-room mountaintop cabins, dispensing love potions and tonics. Well, she acknowledged, it wouldn't hurt if he was suspicious of her. That was a lot easier to deal with than desire. Anything was easier to deal with than desire. Desire frightened her.

"Would you like to come in and walk around?" she offered hesitantly. Wearing a conservative European-tailored suit and hand-tooled Italian leather shoes, he wasn't exactly dressed for a greenhouse. But he did look good, Caitlin had to admit, though she tried not to notice how good.

"Yes," Max said, "I would." It might be best if he investigated this herbal business very carefully before deciding whether or not to take on the job. Although, working on Love, Inc., could have its advantages, he decided as Caitlin turned and headed toward the door, her firm bottom swaying from side to side.

The reason for the peculiar arching roof became apparent when they entered. It was made of transparent heavyweight plastic shaded only by an open-weave cloth so dappled sunlight reached every corner of the interior. Gravel covered the floor and long benches supported hundreds, perhaps thousands, of potted plants. Floor-to-ceiling shelves stacked with bags and cartons lined one end of the building.

"The office is back here." Caitlin led the way to the far corner.

Max picked his way across what amounted to a small obstacle course comprised of tables, lengths of watering hoses, and bags of potting soil. He didn't want to think about what the gravel was doing to the soles of his shoes. But things were well organized, he thought. Considering. All the plants were lined up in neat, labeled rows, each with its own watering siphon. All the packages on the shelves were marked and organized alphabetically.

The office was another matter altogether, and Max groaned inwardly when he saw it. No wonder her accountant had threatened to walk out. It was a wall-to-wall disaster. A small mountain of paper adorned the top of the lone file cabinet. A whole mountain range marched across what he could only suppose was the desk. Assorted cardboard boxes filled with more papers were stacked on the floor. Mail covered half the telephone and he saw the cord to what he assumed was a calculator hanging off the end of the desk. The calculator itself was completely buried. He'd have to take this job, Max told himself. She needed him.

She was entirely too gorgeous and distracting, however. Something told him that she was the kind of woman he could get involved with and he feared getting involved. He could ill afford to be, especially after Jackie. He couldn't afford the emotional energy, and he couldn't afford it financially.

The company was the one thing Jackie hadn't gotten away from him, and for the past two years he'd put his heart and soul into it. The first six months after the divorce, he'd even slept in his office. Partly out of dedication, but mostly because he couldn't afford the rent for an apartment. Almost everything he earned he'd channeled back into the business. Even the expensive suit and nice car were business related. After all, an efficiency consultant needed to project a successful image.

He was doing well now. So well that he could give this assignment to any one of several people working for him—Michael, maybe, or Emily Jane. No, not Michael. He was too slick, a bit of a ladies' man. Max didn't want him around Caitlin. He'd give it to Emily Jane instead.

"Well, what do you think?" Caitlin asked. "Is it hopeless?"

"Not at all," he replied. "But I think it will require my personal attention." Damnation! So much for giving it to Emily Jane. "First I need to find out what it is you're looking for from Shore Efficiency Consultants, what it is you want us to do."

"I need help in organizing my office. You can feel free to do it any way you like. I just have to have really good record-keeping." Caitlin sighed. "The IRS audited me this year and I couldn't find half my receipts. That's why my accountant rebelled."

I shouldn't wonder, Max thought, casting another glance around the office. "We should be able to organize it and set up a record-keeping system in just a week or two. I'd like to meet with your office personnel this Friday, if I could, to discuss present office procedures."

"You've already met with my office personnel," Caitlin said dryly.

"You're it?"

"I'm it."

"Ah, right." Max paused. "Would it be okay if I spent a day or two looking over everything?"

"I—that would be fine," Caitlin murmured even as she thought that he was too disturbing to have hanging around, even for a day or two.

She made a mistake then and looked up directly into his eyes. There were blues and there were blues—slate blues, baby blues, cornflower blues, navy blues. But she didn't think anyone had ever coined a name for the blue of his eyes. And those eyes were currently darkened with hazy appreciation. Caitlin swallowed hard, her gaze glued to his. Her heart began to pound and she felt breathless.

The moment was full of tension and attraction,

wonder and fear. It was also over quickly because Jordan tugged on Max's sleeve. "Mr. Shore, next time you come back, can I talk on your car phone? Can I? Please?"

With relief Caitlin turned away from that mesmerizing gaze and admonished her son. "Jordan. Mr. Shore doesn't have time for—"

"Sure you can," Max interjected smoothly. "Who would you like to call?"

"My best friend, Patrick. Boy, he won't believe that I'm calling him from a car phone!" Jordan continued to chatter on as he followed Caitlin and Max to the front door.

"Um, thank you for taking me on as a client," Caitlin said, feeling uncomfortable. "I—uh, I guess I'll see you Friday. Well, good-bye." She shut the door a little too hastily, but couldn't shut out the memories of unfathomable blue eyes.

Although Caitlin spent the rest of the afternoon cataloging a new shipment, thoughts of a different kind occupied her mind. Maximillian Shore. He made her aware of her own femininity in a way she hadn't been in a long time. As a matter of fact, it had been a long time since her best friend Donna had accused her of exiling herself to a sexual and emotional desert.

Maybe she had, she admitted to herself, but it was a lot safer that way. She didn't take chances. What frightened her about Max Shore was that he made her feel as if she wanted to.

With her thoughts in such a jumble, Caitlin wasn't in the mood for the boisterous dinner that evening. If it weren't for Jordie, she'd have called Donna and begged off from going over. But one of Donna's sons was Patrick and Jordie had been looking forward to seeing him all day.

After the meal the kids were dispatched upstairs to play video games while Caitlin and Donna took glasses of lemonade into the living room.

"I meant to ask you earlier, how did the meeting go yesterday with the IRS?"

"I got off pretty lucky, considering. But Arnie told me in no uncertain terms that unless I called in somebody to organize the office and records, he was going to quit."

"Boy, if sweet li'l ol' Arnie said that, I'd take him seriously."

"Oh, I did. I called an efficiency expert yesterday afternoon. He came by today to look over the business. He said they should be able to get things in decent shape in a couple of weeks."

"A couple of weeks in a pig's eye!" retorted Donna. "Don't forget, I've seen your office. What I don't understand is how you've managed not to lose a few bills in all that mess."

"I pay 'em as I get 'em, that's why. I have to. I know paperwork's not my strong point. It's a miracle I ever made it through college."

Donna snorted. "Having a nearly photographic memory didn't hurt."

Caitlin fell silent. She did have an extraordinarily good memory, and it wasn't always a blessing. There were a few things she wished she could forget. Although she liked her memories of Max Shore's eyes. Mentally she catalogued all the blues she could think of: lapis lazuli; forget-me-nots; her son's favorite Braves baseball cap . . .

"Hello. Anybody in there?"

"Hmm? What?" The glittering blue eyes in her memory gave way to reality.

"Where were you, Caitlin?"

"Oh, um, sorry, Donna. Just daydreaming."

"About who?" Donna teased.

To her chagrin, Caitlin could feel the flush that crept up her cheeks.

"Aha!" Donna said with glee. "There *is* somebody! It's about time!"

"No, there isn't," Caitlin protested.

"Who is he?"

"No one. I mean, I only just met—" Caitlin broke off abruptly, realizing that she'd given herself away. Now Donna would never give up. "C'mon, Donna. Just let it drop, okay?"

"No way," Donna stated. "You going to tell me or what?"

"There's nothing to tell. Really." She protested weakly, but Caitlin knew Donna was going to worry this the rest of the night like a terrier with a bone.

"I repeat. Who is he?"

Caitlin gave up. "His name is Max Shore," she said reluctantly. "He's the owner of the consulting firm I called."

"And?" Donna leaned forward, her eyes gleaming.

"And nothing."

"Did he ask you out?"

"No. And if he did, I wouldn't go. You know I don't date much." Caitlin stood and walked over to the window, looking out at the night, but seeing only old images in her mind.

"Yeah, and the guys you do date could all qualify for the Caspar Milquetoast of the Year Award. You haven't been out with an honest-to-God sexy man in years. How about this Max Shore? Is he sexy?"

Caitlin let out a heartfelt "Yes. A little stuffy, but

definitely sexy." Memories teased her—of Max's broad shoulders, thick, soft-looking hair, long legs—and always those warm, enigmatic, intriguing blue eyes.

"Then go for it, why don't you?"

With an effort Caitlin snapped her attention back to Donna. "I can't." She lifted troubled eyes to her friend. "Donna, you know exactly what I've been through. It's taken me all of these past seven years to put my life back together."

"But you did. That's what counts," Donna said gently.

"Oh, I did all right. But there are times I feel as if I'm held together with paper clips and rubber bands. I'm scared to do anything to rock the boat."

Donna was silent for a moment, then said, "I know you're scared. But what happened to you happened a long time ago and you can't let it color the rest of your life. Find a man—a real man. Get married. Settle down. Or don't settle down, have a passionate affair. Whatever you do, you've got to let go of the past."

"I don't know if I can." Caitlin's voice was the barest whisper. "Oh, Donna, I don't know if I can."

Two

Maximillian Shore will be at the greenhouse today, Caitlin thought the minute she awakened. She still wasn't sure if she liked the idea. Nonetheless, after she scurried Jordan out the door to the waiting school bus, she took extra care dressing for work.

Instead of the usual faded jeans and T-shirt, she wore newer black denims and a spring-green blouse. She harnessed her unruly shoulder-length blond curls into a topknot, but despite all her efforts, dozens of little tendrils escaped to spiral softly about her face. She even brushed a light coat of mascara over her lashes. Here goes nothing, she thought as she grabbed her purse and headed to her van.

As luck would have it, unusually slow traffic made Caitlin fifteen minutes late, and she saw Max already standing by the greenhouse door when she pulled into the parking lot. She should have known that an efficiency expert would not only be on time, but would be looking at his watch. He appeared elegant—and, again, too conventional—in another suit and tie. Perhaps she should tell him that there was no air-conditioning in the greenhouse and by midafternoon, with the late April sun streaming in, it could get pretty warm.

"You're late," Max said flatly.

Caitlin bit back the apology she'd been ready to offer. On second thought, she wouldn't tell him about the heat. Let him cook in his dull little suit. She gave a saccharine smile. "Good morning to you too, Mr. Shore."

"The first thing I want to do this morning is go over your standard office procedure with you," Max said as soon as they walked inside the building.

"Well," Caitlin retorted mildly, "the first thing *I'm* going to do is water the back third of the greenhouse. Perhaps you could familiarize yourself with my office while you're waiting."

Max sighed. "Fine. Then—"

"Then I'm going to water the middle third. Then I'm going to water the front third."

"Can any of that wait?"

"No, it can't. Plants wilt. People don't." With that parting shot, she spun on her heels and walked to the back of the building.

Max frowned as he watched her. Damn! Did he have to start off this morning by snapping at her? He didn't know why he'd done it. One minute he'd been thinking how good she looked; the next minute a curt "You're late!" popped out of his mouth. Maybe some ancient deep-rooted sense of male self-preservation had caused it, he thought ruefully. Though she hadn't exactly been the soul of graciousness either. She'd been tart, even testy.

Was this the same woman who'd been haunting his dreams? Max couldn't understand it. He had always preferred his women soft and compliant and classy. So what attracted him to this sarcastic pint-sized Attila the Hun who dressed like a teenage refugee? Hell, she was probably married. He frowned at the thought. She wore no ring, he'd noticed, but then, she was also cussedly independent, perhaps she simply chose not to. Max frowned again and headed to the office. This day wasn't turning out at all as he'd hoped.

When he opened the office door, the same mess still waited, with the addition of another couple of layers of mail. He sure had his work cut out for him. Max shook his head, wondering if Caitlin ever filed anything. When he decided to check the file cabinet, he saw the largest cat he'd ever seen lounging on top of it.

"Hello, kitty." Max reached out a friendly hand, only to draw it back when the cat met him with an ill-tempered growl. "Sorry." Max decided to start with the desk instead.

Caitlin turned on the automatic watering system, then went down the rows and double-checked that every plant was hooked up properly. She'd followed this routine every day for months, ever since she had gotten the siphon system, but today her thoughts weren't with her work. They were in her office with Maximillian Shore. At least Max had decided to be grumpy this morning. It would be much easier to keep her distance. And Lord knew she had to.

She couldn't avoid him forever, however tempting the idea. She had to go into that office sometime. It was a shame it wasn't any bigger. The thought of being closed up in that tiny space with

Max unnerved her. And, she reluctantly admitted, excited her. He reeked of masculinity and made her feel soft and womanly and vulnerable in response. Only she didn't want to feel vulnerable. Not ever again.

After an hour Caitlin entered the dreary office and paused in shock. Max had miraculously cleared off the top of the desk. Three days worth of mail had even been opened and sorted—bills, invoices, and purchase agreements were in separate stacks. "Wow, I'm impressed."

He shrugged well-muscled shoulders. "It'll take another few days to get things together. But getting anything organized is the easy part. Keeping it organized is the hard part. That's what I'm here to do. Together we'll come up with a workable system. Right now I'd like to mention just a few things. If you have the time, that is." His voice was carefully neutral.

Caitlin squirmed a little. She had been touchy all morning. It wasn't his fault that he put her on edge. "I'm sorry," she said quickly. "I should have told you the other day that mornings are pretty hectic around here. I have plants to water, and they can't wait. Friday mornings are even busier because I have calls to make and orders to get together to be shipped on Mondays. Today's even worse than usual because Martha's been out sick all week." She smiled.

From Attila the Hun to an angel, and all it took was that smile. He could spend the rest of his life watching that smile. Whoa! Where'd *that* idea come from? Max hurriedly reined in his wandering mind. "I, ah, made a list of some items you'll need to get your office in order. I usually deal with an office equipment warehouse across town, but if you know someone else who can give you a better price, go ahead."

"Just what kind of equipment are we talking about?" Caitlin said warily as she mentally added up the balance in the company checking account.

Max took out a small notebook from his shirt pocket and began reading. "One four-drawer file cabinet, a decent calculator, a stapler, blue and red pens—" Max glanced up. "Do you realize you have only one pen, and a green one at that?"

"I like green," Caitlin muttered. "Go on. What else?"

"Legal pads, manila file folders, a Rolodex, a proper ledger book—"

"Anything else?" Caitlin interrupted.

"Just one more thing. I'd highly recommend a computer."

"A computer?" Absolutely not! It wasn't just the expense. Caitlin hated machines, even cars. She and her van had an uneasy agreement. As long as it got her where she wanted to go, she didn't junk it. She didn't have any kind of an agreement with computers. She hated them and they hated her. With horrified fascination, Caitlin listened as Max began to wax positively lyrical about computers.

". . . And they can streamline your bookkeeping system and invoicing methods. They can even handle payroll."

"No need for that," Caitlin said. "There are just three other employees."

Max went on as if he hadn't heard. ". . . And they can keep a running inventory."

"No computer."

"Look, I know it's a pretty big initial investment, but it's worth it. Even a small personal computer can save hundreds of man-hours."

"No computer."

"But they're efficient and they will eliminate the possibility of human error."

"I *like* human error. What I don't like is computer error." Caitlin was emphatic.

She should have known that an efficiency expert would be gung-ho on computers. She had promised Arnie that she'd take the consultant's advice, but she'd fight Max fang and claw over this. She'd better make her position clear right now, because heaven help her if Max mentioned it to Arnie. Arnie would go for it all the way. "Absolutely no computer, Mr. Shore. Zip, zero, zilch."

"Okay, okay. Don't get so hot about it."

"I'm not hot about it!" Caitlin found herself nearly shouting in response. She paused in shock. She hadn't shouted in years. She'd always kept her emotions on an even keel, preferring not to feel anything too intensely. But there was something about Max Shore that set her teeth on edge. Actually, it set her whole body on edge.

Feeling uncomfortable, Caitlin turned away and began stroking the cat still lying across the file cabinet. The cat purred, a loud deep rumble of pleasure, and rolled on his back.

"I'll be damned!" Max said softly and, when Caitlin lifted puzzled eyes to his, continued. "All that cat has done this morning is growl and hiss at me."

"Charlemagne? He wouldn't hurt a flea."

"Not a flea, maybe, but I'll bet he can lick his weight in pit bulls," Max muttered, then felt a little ridiculous. The cat looked soft and boneless as he lay sprawled on his back, getting his tummy rubbed. He reached out his hand, but no sooner had he touched the cat's head than the cat grabbed Max's hand with his claws and growled, daring Max to trespass farther.

Caitlin murmured, "Gee. All these years I've never known he was an attack cat."

"Well, now you know. Would you mind calling him off?"

"He'd only ignore me. Charlemagne's pretty much a law unto himself." Caitlin felt a smug satisfaction. Max was well and truly caught. As long as he didn't move his hand, Charlemagne was content merely to hold it. Whenever Max tried to move his fingers, the cat renewed his attack.

"So what do I do now? Stand here all day waiting until this cat gets tired?"

He could stand there all day, she thought suddenly, and she wouldn't mind a bit. He had a nice back—muscular without being bumpy, and if she were the type of woman to notice a man's derriere, then she'd certainly notice the way the fabric of his trousers pulled across his tight bottom. However, she wasn't the type.

She cleared her throat. "Not all day, but if you'd wait just a minute . . ." Caitlin tore a long strip of paper from the notepad on the desk and wiggled that in front of Charlemagne. The cat's ears stood at attention and his tail twitched before he reached out a paw to bat at the paper. Max stole the opportunity to jerk his hand away and glanced down at it. "See? He left me scarred."

Without thinking, Caitlin reached over and gently took his hand to look at the barely visible pinpricks. "They're hardly noticeable at all," she said, her fingertips brushing over his skin. "Next time . . ."

Her voice died as Max's hand wrapped around hers, leaving it warm and tingling. Caitlin looked up then, her brown eyes meeting his blue ones. His fingers threaded through hers when her tongue slipped out to moisten her lips. The sudden hunger that flared in the depths of his gaze caught her by surprise. She jerked loose and took a step back.

Max noticed the anxious expression on Caitlin's face. For a moment she had looked as lost and as scared as a child who couldn't find her mother. What had frightened her? Was it him? Or the sudden desire that had loomed between them? Whatever the cause, the fear in her eyes made Max want to enfold her in his arms and promise her she'd always be safe.

Caitlin spun away and busily flipped through a stack of invoices on the desk. Perhaps it would be best to ignore the whole thing, she thought. "I know you want to run down office procedures with me this morning, but would it be okay if we did that this afternoon? I have a few calls to make right now, and K.C. will be here after lunch to look after the place."

"That would be fine. If you could move that cat, I'll even look at reorganizing the filing system." Max pulled a pristine white handkerchief from his back pocket and wiped a thin film of sweat from his forehead."Is it always this warm in here?"

"Not always." Caitlin gave a small smile. "Usually it's worse."

"Worse?"

"Worse. I do have a ventilation system out in the greenhouse that keeps the temperature from getting above ninety, but it doesn't help much in here."

"You're telling me," Max grumbled as he loosened his necktie.

Caitlin watched, captivated, as Max proceeded to unbutton his shirt-sleeves and roll up the cuffs, revealing forearms that were tanned and well-muscled. When he began on the top buttons of his shirt, she mumbled, "I'm going to put on the fans," then turned to leave.

"Ah, before you go, would you mind taking the cat with you?"

"It probably won't help much." Caitlin hoisted the cat in her arms, the huge beast dangling as limply as overcooked spaghetti. "He can open the office door by himself."

"Does he live in the greenhouse?"

"Sometimes. Sometimes he follows me out to the van when I'm ready to leave. That's when I know he wants to go home with me. In other words, he decides where he wants to be." Caitlin switched the heavy animal to her other arm, carefully avoiding meeting Max's eyes.

"I guess Jordan, or, ah, your husband isn't allergic to cats." Was it obvious to her that he was fishing for information on her marital status?

"Neither Jordan nor I are allergic to cats."

She hadn't mentioned a husband, Max thought in relief. Surely, if she were married, she'd have said something about her husband. "Hmm? What?" Max realized that Caitlin had been speaking to him.

"I said," she repeated patiently, "that I'm going to take care of my calls now. I usually eat lunch around twelve-thirty or one. You're welcome to join me if you like."

"That would be fine, thanks. Would you like me to order something?" Max asked, thinking of Super Subs with their deluxe heros piled high with hot peppers or Piggy's Pizza and its everything-but-the-kitchen-sink pizza.

"If you don't mind." Caitlin smiled. "There's a terrific place just a couple of blocks away that delivers. The number is on the green label stuck on the side of the telephone."

When she had left the office, Max called the number, only to be told the day's specials included grilled tofu with lemon, tabouli with chopped walnuts, and hummus sandwiches. Lord, no, Max thought. He wasn't going to order that slop. It wasn't even fit for an animal. Well, he amended, thinking of Charlemagne, maybe for one animal. Wasn't it nice of Caitlin, though, to order from them just because they happened to be close. However, nice was one thing Max wasn't when it came to his food. He'd order in some real dishes, he thought with satisfaction. Caitlin would probably appreciate a decent meal.

Caitlin spent the next hour in the back of the greenhouse at the phone extension, trying to track down American ginseng. As she hung up after finalizing an order for eighty pounds, she felt the back of her neck prickle and turned to see Max standing behind her, watching her. She wondered how long he'd been there. "Hi," she said, feeling somewhat shy.

"Lunch is in the office."

"Um, thanks. I'll be right in." Caitlin turned, walked over to the sink, and rinsed her hands. She hoped Max had gotten the tabouli. The Garden made really great tabouli. The grilled tofu sandwiches weren't bad either, and the house salad with yogurt dressing was outstanding. Her mouth watering, she pushed open the door to the office.

She nearly groaned aloud, her appetite shrinking like a wool sweater in hot water. Chinese food. She couldn't eat Chinese food. It wasn't just that it happened to be sweet and sour pork—she didn't eat meat—but it had lots of monosodium glutamate. Monosodium glutamate gave her hives. She was about ready to tell Max, when she saw how neatly everything was arranged. The desk was cleared and plates, along with napkins, set in place as carefully as if they were china and not just paper.

He had gone to great pains, and Caitlin couldn't bring herself to say anything except "Oh, you shouldn't have gone to so much trouble." In fact, she wished he hadn't.

"It was no trouble at all," he replied cheerfully. "I thought this would be something we could both enjoy."

When he smiled that boyish yet disturbingly masculine smile, Caitlin resigned herself to a long night of itching.

Lunch was quiet as Max ate with enthusiasm and Caitlin unobtrusively picked out the green pepper and pineapple, leaving the pork on the plate. After the meal Caitlin explained her general office procedure—or more precisely, her lack of it. To Max's credit, he said nothing, though had he been the type to raise his eyebrows, they would have long since disappeared beneath the thatch of hair that fell across his brow.

Interesting, he thought more than once over the course of the afternoon, Caitlin seemed to make a concerted effort *not* to be organized. After all, in an office as small as hers, it wouldn't be any more trouble to tuck something in a folder than it was to dig through stacks of paper for it. As a matter of fact, it would be less.

Considering how carefully she tried to control her feelings, it was an interesting contradiction. Perhaps, he mused, she wasn't as controlled as she wanted everyone to think. Maybe she was trying to suppress a creative, passionate nature and the sloppiness and lack of organization were simply outlets for those stifled emotions. A sudden jolt ran through Max, and he knew he wanted to be there the day she gave her creativity and passion free rein.

He had one more piece to the puzzle that was Caitlin, a puzzle that he desperately yearned to put together. Most of all, he wanted to figure out why she avoided physical contact. Was it him in particular or contact in general? In the office it was next to impossible to move around without brushing by each other. But instead of saying a friendly "excuse me," Caitlin would lower her eyes and draw in her breath.

When K.C. came in at one-thirty, Max discovered that it wasn't just him after all. K.C., a tall, gangly teenage boy, burst through the office door with a whoop. He grabbed Caitlin and swung her around while yelling something about a girl named Diana and Friday night. No sooner had he set Caitlin down than Max saw her run a trembling hand through her hair.

"Goodness, K.C.!" she exclaimed with a smile, even though Max could swear to a slight tremor in her voice. "You want to calm down and say it in plain English?"

"She said, yes, Caitlin. We're going out Friday night."

"That's terrific. Where are you going to take her?"

"Gosh, I hadn't thought about that." He paused, frowning. "It'll have to be someplace kinda classy, but not too classy. Don't want it to look like I'm showing off, you know. Maybe we could go to the . . ." Still muttering to himself, he stalked through the office door and headed toward the back of the greenhouse.

"Hey, wait!" Caitlin called after him. "How's your mom feeling?" K.C. was Martha's son.

"Better," he hollered back.

Caitlin turned to Max with an apologetic shrug. "Sorry about the interruption. But K.C. has had a crush on Diana since he met her last summer. This date is the culmination of a year's worth of work." She reached up a hand and absently scratched the back of her neck. "Anyway, let's get back to this."

While Max went over a rudimentary filing system, his brain busily catalogued a new fact about Ms. Caitlin Alexandra Love. It wasn't just that she disliked being touched. He'd met a few people before who simply disliked too-familiar physical contact. No, Caitlin feared it. Max was taken aback by the way this made him feel—fiercely protective of her and violently angry at who or what had caused her to become this way.

He kept casting covert glances at her, and every time she met his eye, she squirmed uncomfortably and rubbed her arms. He made her nervous—or so it seemed to him until she reached across to get a pencil, and he saw angry red patches beginning to show on her forearms. "Good Lord!" he exclaimed as he leaned over and grasped the arm she was carelessly scratching. "What's this?"

Caitlin looked down and, even though she'd been expecting it, blinked when she saw the characteristic blotches of hives all over her left arm. She'd been so engrossed listening to Max that she'd hardly noticed the itching had started. "Oh, um"—she tried without success to extricate her arm from his hold—"it's nothing. Just hives."

"Just hives? It looks awful. Don't you have anything to put on it?"

"I have some cream in my purse. I'll just get it and—"

Without releasing her, Max snared the shoulder strap of her purse from her chair. He hauled it across the desk and unceremoniously dumped the contents out, zeroing in on the tube of prescription cream. He released her arm only long enough to uncap the tube and squeeze a generous amount into the palm of his hand. Grabbing her arm again, he began to apply the cream in long, smooth strokes.

"No, I'll put it on," Caitlin said quickly, but he ignored her and continued to massage in the cream. Her skin tingled everywhere he touched it and her left hand and wrist felt peculiarly weak and languid. Her breath seemed to catch in her throat. As a matter of fact, she couldn't take a normal breath at all until Max let go of her arm.

She drew in air only to have it catch again when Max took the other arm into his gentle hands and began to apply the cream. The characteristic panic that normally set in at close contact loomed its ugly head, but subsided under the almost mesmerizing rhythm of his stroking.

It felt so good, so right to touch her, Max thought hazily as his hands caressed her forearms. And whether she knew it or not, she was a woman who needed to be touched often. But in the right way and by the right man. And *he* was the right man.

Shocked by what he was thinking, he released her abruptly. "I, uh, think I'll go outside for a few minutes and walk around. It's got to be cooler out there than in here."

Yeah, in more ways than one, Caitlin thought, absently running her fingers over the arm he'd been caressing. No, she corrected herself, he'd been massaging in allergy cream. If his touch had felt unusually good, it was only because the cream was so cool and soothing. With a decisive nod Caitlin turned and picked up the telephone, now easily found on the cleared desk.

She was in the middle of a detailed conversation when Max reentered the office. Her eyes met his and she paused in the middle of a sentence, then made a concerted effort to get her scattered thoughts back together. "Um, I beg your pardon, Luther, could you repeat that last price again?"

She hastily scribbled something on a scrap of paper. "Well, thanks, and if you come across a source on the Salix alba, give me a call. . . . No, I don't want the Salix purpurea. . . . Well, because my customer doesn't want the purpurea. . . . Let's face it, Luther, in our line of work you give the customer what he wants, and what he wants is the alba. . . . Thanks again."

"May I ask what Salix alba is?"

She made an effort not to meet his gaze again. "It's willow bark. White willow, to be precise. It's used for medicinal purposes."

"What for?" Max sounded skeptical.

"For pain relief."

"Why not take an aspirin?" Max asked reasonably.

"Willow bark contains salicin, which converts to salicylic acid in the body. Salicylic acid is the major component in aspirin."

"So, why not take an aspirin?" Max repeated.

"Because," Caitlin explained patiently, "some people don't want man-made chemicals cluttering up their bodies."

"Is this what you take when you have a headache?"

"No." Smiling, Caitlin finally looked up at him. "I take aspirin."

Max gave an answering grin, then sobered and murmured, "You know, you're one beautiful lady when you smile." He reached out a hand and ran it down her cheek.

Caitlin's smile faltered, then faded altogether under his scrutiny. Without thinking, she pressed her cheek into his palm and ran her tongue over her lips, all the while gazing into his eyes. Such a blue, she thought. Robin's-egg blue, periwinkle blue . . . She trailed off as she saw the message in his eyes. He was going to kiss her. His head tilted to one side as his hand cupped her cheek, his thumb running over her bottom lip.

She felt her breasts swell and tingle, and a strange warmth pooled in her abdomen. Wordlessly, she waited, mesmerized by the sudden flame that sparked to life in his gaze. But as he bent his head toward hers, that old familiar demon she'd lived with for seven years loomed in her mind. Its dark shadow blotted out everything but the fear that always lurked nearby.

Her sharply indrawn breath and the sudden stiffening of her body let Max know he'd moved too fast. Someday, sweet Cait, he thought. Someday soon. He let his hand drop and said with a studied casualness, "Well, I need to be going now. I have to check back in at the office before it gets too late. Did you need the address of that office supply warehouse we discussed?"

At Caitlin's bemused nod he fished through his wallet and pulled out a card. "Ask for Donald and tell him you're there at my recommendation. He'll give you a discount. See you on Monday." Max gave a jaunty smile and left, feeling pleased with his acting ability.

In total bewilderment Caitlin stared at the doorway he'd just walked through. Had she read him wrong? She must have, because she could have sworn he'd intended to kiss her. She leaned back against the edge of the desk, her heart still pounding, and shook her head, torn between relief and disappointment. What a strange man, she thought. Strange and nerve-racking. And intriguing.

Three

"That'll be fine. See you then." Caitlin hung up the telephone and smiled at the receiver. It was certainly kind of Max to offer to run by her house with some papers for her to sign. With dawning horror she looked down at herself. Not only was her house a disaster, but so was she. She'd been working in her yard and was hot and sweaty and dirty.

Why hadn't he called when she and Jordan had just gotten home from Sunday school a couple of hours earlier, perfectly groomed and dressed to the hilt? Now she looked like somebody's disreputable kid brother, in torn jeans, baggy sweatshirt, and dilapidated sneakers. Grass stains, garden soils, and a fine layer of the pulverized lime she'd been applying to her lawn covered almost all of her.

She didn't have time to clean both the house and herself, so which would it be? Caitlin thought of her living room. At one end of the sofa, a stack of laundry sat, waiting to be put away. The Sunday paper was strewn across the coffee table and the floor—whatever floor space wasn't covered with Lego building bricks—and at least two dirty juice glasses cluttered the top of a dusty television.

Then Caitlin glanced down at herself and made her decision. The living room would just have to look lived in.

Caitlin hastily put away her yard tools and hurried to the bathroom. "Jordie?" she called out as she turned on the shower. "Come down to the living room and scrape up your Legos and put them away. Okay?"

"Aw, Mom, I'm building something. Can't I do it later?"

"Jordie, please. Mr. Shore is dropping by in a little while. He's not used to kids. He'll kill himself walking across the living room. Now, get them up, okay?"

"But Mom—"

"Jordan Reynolds Love, I said now, please." Caitlin waited until she heard grudging footsteps coming down the stairs before closing the bathroom door and hurriedly stepping into the shower.

She was toweling her hair dry when she heard Jordan's muffled voice through the door. "I can't hear you, honey," she called. "I'll be out in a minute." Tucking a towel securely around her, she opened the door and walked into the living room. "Jordan? What—?" She stopped short.

Seated on the sofa, Max had been surveying the cluttered surroundings, and when he saw Caitlin his mouth went dry. Lord, she was beautiful all over. Her damp hair hung in burnished gold ringlets, giving her a little-girl look. The full breasts straining at the towel were anything but a little girl's, however. And her legs—beautiful legs, gorgeous legs, legs meant to be wrapped around a man's waist.

Her skin was the color of rich cream and shone with thousands of water droplets that were like dew on a white rose, Max thought. A sharp pang of hunger shot through him, bringing him to his feet. "Caitlin," he began, then stopped at the dry husky sound of his voice.

"What are you doing here?" Caitlin squeaked. "You're early." Then she added, "Where's Jordan?"

"He, ah, said to tell you he was going to get Jerry and show him my car phone." Max's eyes fastened with hungry fascination on the rosy blush that began at the top of her breasts and spread rapidly up her cheeks. He reached out a hand to trace the path of an errant drop of water that slid sinuously down over her collarbone.

Breathlessly Caitlin looked down and watched his fingers. Licking suddenly dry lips, she stepped away. "Well, if you'll excuse me," Caitlin said with as much dignity as she could muster under the circumstances, "I'll go get dressed."

A smile, both boyish and wicked, lit Max's face. "Oh, don't bother on my account."

"I'm doing it on my own account," Caitlin muttered as she walked down the hall to her bedroom. "I don't want to catch a chill from the draft."

When Caitlin entered the living room a few minutes later, she wore white cotton slacks—just so he'd know she didn't always wear jeans—and a yellow scoop-neck T-shirt. Yellow clips held her damp hair back from her face. She hoped she looked as poised and collected as he did in his navy suit, white shirt, and burgundy striped tie.

Didn't he ever wear anything but suits? Caitlin found herself wondering.

Still preoccupied with remembering what Caitlin had looked like a few minutes before, Max hardly noticed what she wore now. He'd better think about her in that towel later, in private, he realized as the fit of his trousers became a little less comfortable. He shifted position.

"Ah, Caitlin . . ." He paused as his mind searched desperately for the reason he'd dropped by. Oh, yeah. "I have a copy of our standard contract for you to sign. The fee we discussed is listed on the second page. If you'd like to take a day or two to go over it with your attorney, please feel free." And if you want to take a year or two to go over anything at all with me, feel free to do that too, he found himself thinking wistfully.

Caitlin wasn't in the frame of mind to go over important business details. She couldn't give them the attention they needed when Max Shore and the look in his eye preoccupied her. A hot flicker in the blue depths said that he remembered exactly how she appeared less clothed. And that he approved wholeheartedly.

She wondered fancifully how Max would look wrapped in only a towel. His usually conservative hair would be mussed, and the curls of hair on his chest would be glistening with water droplets. An arrow of hair would disappear under the edge of the towel and . . .

She took a deep breath. "I believe I will," she said quickly. "I mean, I'd like to have my attorney look it over." Not that she had an attorney, but if Max thought she should have one, then so be it.

Caitlin got to her feet and stepped over to the front door. "Well, thank you, Mr. Shore, er, Max, for bringing these by. I'll have them ready for you in a day or two," she said in a tone of dismissal, then paused, waiting for him to take the hint and leave.

Max leaned back on the sofa, crossing his arms and looking quite at home. "As long as you're up," he said, "could I have a glass of water? It's quite warm today, don't you think?"

Caitlin took another deep breath to calm her nerves. "Perhaps you'd like iced tea or fruit juice instead," she offered, managing to sound courteous but cool.

"Great," Max said with a smile. "Either one. I'm not picky." He could see through her transparent attempt to get rid of him. He had news for her. He wasn't going anywhere.

Disgruntled, Caitlin walked into the kitchen. She'd have thought he'd have taken the hint. He wasn't so dense that the hint escaped him. He was so pigheaded he chose to ignore it.

"Either one. I'm not picky," she mimicked as she squeezed a slice of lemon into his tea. He was so stubborn! she thought as she absently squeezed another slice of lemon. She'd done everything but ask him to leave, but he'd apparently decided to get on her nerves instead. She squeezed a third slice, then a fourth, puzzling over how one man could be so irritating.

She would just irritate him right back if he tried anything else, she decided as she carried the glass to him.

Eve with her apple, Max thought as he stood and accepted the drink from her outstretched hand. He took a long swallow, nearly choking as the sour liquid, unrelieved by even a few grains of sugar, went down his throat. He managed to retain a straight face, however, and even gave her a bland smile as he took another sip, better prepared this time for the acidity. "Just what I needed," he murmured, fixing an intent gaze on her. "A little tea with my lemon."

Caitlin's face reddened with embarrassment as she suddenly noticed the large number of lemon slices floating in his glass. Now, how had that happened? She squirmed beneath his scrutiny. She honestly hadn't meant to do that, but there was something about him that chased her brains and good sense right out the window. He'd never believe she hadn't done it on purpose, she realized as his eyes narrowed slightly.

From the look on his face, he was either contemplating dismembering her or kissing her. She didn't know which alternative she preferred. But when he murmured something about needing a little sweetness, she knew which one he'd decided on.

Eyes wide, she felt her heartbeat quicken and her limbs become liquid as he slid a hand, ever so gently, behind her neck. His actions were slow and deliberate, as if he knew that a sudden move would make her bolt. His thumb toyed with her earlobe while his fingers laced through her still-damp hair.

His eyes—were they indigo? cerulean?—caressed her lips in a kiss almost as potent as the real thing. Certainly the real thing could not have sent her heart racing any faster or caused her face to flush any hotter. Caitlin stiffened, waiting for her old companion, panic, to barge in. Strangely, it seemed to be held at bay by the warmth radiating from wherever he touched her.

"Mom? Mr. Shore? Jerry's here. Can we see

your car phone?" Jordan yelled as he and his friend walked in the front door.

With a look that said this wasn't over by a long shot, Max turned a smile to the two small boys. "Sure, Jordan. Hi, Jerry." Shaking the tow-headed boy's hand, he said, "I'm Max Shore," then took the two excited boys out to his car.

Caitlin sat down abruptly as the screen door shut, and stared at the glass of tea Max had set down on the table. She realized just then that she hadn't been afraid. When he touched her, an odd sort of breathlessness had set in, and a strange warmth had rendered her limbs all but useless. But no fear. No panic. Somehow, that scared her more than anything else.

Max spent over an hour outside with the two exuberant boys. Every time Caitlin peeked out the front door, either Jerry or Jordan would be talking animatedly on the telephone, and Max would be leaning against the side of the car, an indulgent smile on his face. She ventured out once with glasses of milk and little boxes of raisins for the kids and the rest of Max's tea.

"Your tea," she proffered with a straight face.

"Gee," he said with a teasing smile. "Can't I have milk too?"

"Certainly," Caitlin replied primly, and turned to go back into the house.

"No lemon," he called after her.

Caitlin hurried away before the grin that played about her mouth broke through. She smiled the whole time she poured his milk, especially when she whimsically perched a lemon slice on the rim of the glass.

She did compose herself when she carried the drink out to Max, but one glance at his face when he saw the lemon and she couldn't prevent a giggle from escaping. It was a little rusty from disuse, but a giggle nonetheless.

Max could tell she didn't laugh often and felt bewildered by the sudden tenderness that welled up inside him. He vowed that he would do whatever was necessary to make her laugh, and laugh often. From the shadows that seemed always to lurk in her eyes, he knew that she'd had little enough reason to laugh in her life.

The tenderness showed in his eyes as he held her gaze for a moment, then gave a sudden wink. He took the lemon slice and dropped it into the milk. A long gulp left a milk "mustache" above a boyish grin.

Another giggle broke through and Caitlin rolled her eyes. "You're nuts."

"Certifiable," Max agreed.

"Thanks for letting the boys use your car phone," Caitlin murmured. "I know it'll probably cost you a small fortune, but it's given Jordan something to talk about for the next month." With the late afternoon sun shining down, Caitlin let her gaze linger on the golden highlights glimmering in Max's hair. Streaks of sunshine, she thought fancifully.

"They've gotten more use out of it than I have," he said. "I was thinking of having it taken out. I've used it maybe three times in the year I've had it. It's cost more to keep than it's saved me in time."

"Well, today has meant a lot to Jordan," she said earnestly. "A lot of people make idle promises to kids and think it doesn't matter whether they keep them or not. I'm glad that you made good on yours."

"Hey, I like kids," Max said. "I have three nephews I dote on. The oldest one's about Jordan's age. He's fascinated by the car phone too. His name is Alan. and then there are Matt and Joey. They're four-year-old twin terrors. They're more fascinated with seeing how much trouble they can get into."

They chatted for a few more minutes, then Caitlin went back inside to answer her telephone. It was Donna. Caitlin mentioned the contract and asked if Donna's husband, Rick, would look it over, but decided not to mention the man who'd brought it. Donna would read more into it than there really was. After all, Max Shore was simply a business associate—no more, no less, Caitlin told herself.

She had just hung up when Jordan bounded in, his face wreathed in smiles. "Mom, I had so much fun. Jerry and I called Patrick and Kenny and Jerry's mom and Max even let us talk to somebody at his office. Kenny couldn't believe I talked to him on a car phone and Jerry got on the phone and said I was too. Can he stay for dinner, Mom? I think he's gonna be my best friend."

"Well, I don't see why not, honey. But he needs to check with his mom first, okay?"

"Aw, gee, thanks, Mrs. Love," drawled a very grown-up, and very male voice. "But I think my mom will let me."

Caitlin, who had turned with a start toward the direction of the voice, now turned confused eyes back to Jordan. "Jordie, where's Jerry?"

"He had to go home. He's goin' to his grandma's for dinner. Now, can I take Max up to my room? I wanna show him my new G.I. Joe tank. It's a Cobra vehicle, Max. That's the bad guys. And it has—"

"Wait a minute." Caitlin called a halt. "Jordan, I thought you wanted Jerry to eat dinner with us," she said cautiously.

"Uh-uh. I want Max to. He's my new best friend, Mom. I just told ya," Jordan explained patiently.

"Right," she muttered. "I think I've been had." The feeling intensified when she caught the conspiratorial glance exchanged between the man and the boy. It struck Caitlin how good Max and Jordan were together. Max genuinely liked kids and Jordie knew it and responded with wholehearted acceptance, as only kids can.

Caitlin set about preparing dinner while Jordan took Max up to his room. Her hands absently shaped a mixture of grains, chick peas, and herbs into patties as her ears tuned in to the sounds trickling down the stairs. She could hear Jordan's delighted giggles and chattering punctuated by the occasional rumble of Max's voice. Caitlin's throat tightened as she realized that, had her life been normal, this could have been an average family evening at home.

She resolutely pushed the idea away. Her life had been anything but normal, and the dream of an average family would always be just that—a dream.

Taking a deep breath, she pulled her thoughts back to the task at hand and put the patties in a pan with a splash of olive oil, then turned on the burner. When the patties were done, she hurriedly sliced some whole wheat bread, made sandwiches, and opened a jar of applesauce. This was a favorite meal that she and Jordan had almost every Sunday night.

By the look on Max's face when he entered the kitchen, however, it was obvious that it wasn't going to be *his* favorite meal. He gave a weak smile as he sat, but Caitlin wasn't fooled. What did she expect from someone who liked Chinese food full of monosodium glutamate and little squiggly pieces of pork?

What he did would be interesting to see. Would he make some polite excuse to avoid eating, or would he grin and bear it as she had the Chinese food? Of course, she'd gotten hives for her trouble. She wondered whimsically what Max would get. Keeping an eye on him, she ate her meal and listened with half an ear to Jordan's chatter.

Max pushed the applesauce around on his plate for a while, then subtly lifted the top slice of bread and peeked inside. An Unidentified Fried Object. Well, it looked harmless enough. Gamely, he picked up his sandwich, squeezing the bread a little so he could get it into his mouth. No sooner had he done that than a glob of yogurt mixed with bits of green herbs dropped on the front of his pristine white shirt.

With a sigh Max placed the sandwich back on his plate. He should have known this would happen if he tried to eat something he really didn't like. Unidentified Fried Objects were not on his list of favorite foods. He'd attempted to eat it only out of politeness, and now look at him. He glanced down at the spot with disgust. At least it had missed his silk tie.

"Here." Caitlin handed him a damp paper towel. "If you want to take off your shirt, I'll rinse it in the sink. Yogurt can leave a spot if you don't get it out right away."

When Max's hands loosened his tie and began to unbutton his shirt, Caitlin wished she'd kept her mouth shut. As his shirt fell open, more and more of his chest came into view. It was as richly tanned as the backs of his hands, and glinted with a dusting of the same reddish-gold hair.

When Max shrugged off his shirt, Caitlin felt as if she'd just been blind-sided. The sight of his tanned broad shoulders, muscular arms, and powerful back mesmerized her. She attempted to draw in a deep breath, but there didn't seem to be enough air in the room. She found her eyes tracing the path her hands would have liked to trace, and hastily averted her eyes.

She took the shirt from his hand, walked over to the kitchen sink, and turned on the water. As she scrubbed the stain, she mentally searched through her closets for something for Max to wear. Unfortunately the only things she could come up with that were large enough were a blanket and a man's shirt Caitlin used while painting.

Anything would do at this point, she decided. She just needed to get him covered. And quick. His half-naked torso ruined her concentration and gave her hands a peculiar itchy feeling that she knew would be eased only by touching him.

"Jordan? Would you go upstairs and get my painting shirt?" Caitlin asked as she put Max's shirt in the clothes dryer.

"Oh, don't bother about me," Max said. "I'm fine like I am."

"It's no bother," Caitlin told him quickly. "Jordan, go get the shirt, okay?"

"It's not necessary," Max insisted as Jordan bounded up the stairs.

"Oh, yes, it is," Caitlin muttered. "It's getting a bit cool in here."

"Cool?" Caitlin sure did want to get him dressed quickly, Max thought, then noticed her eyes lingering over his torso. He liked the idea that the sight of his bare chest bothered her. It meant she wasn't indifferent. He decided that he wasn't going to cover up after all. "I don't think it's a bit cool in here. I think it's on the warm side."

Caitlin's eyes met his and saw the challenge there. She never could resist a challenge. "It won't be when I open the windows," she said sweetly.

Max fell silent, though a smile played about his lips. He seemed as determined not to put on a shirt as she was for him to wear one.

Jordan galloped down the stairs and handed Max the old, paint-smeared shirt. "Here's Mom's shirt. It was Patrick's dad's. It's real big."

"Thank you very much, Jordan. I don't need it though," Max said, glancing at Caitlin. "I'm comfortable like I am."

Without saying a word Caitlin opened the kitchen window, hiding a smile as a breeze wafted through the room. It was a normal April night, with temperatures in the low fifties. She couldn't help but notice the gooseflesh appearing on Max's forearms. Surely he'd put that shirt on now, she thought, then wondered why it had become so important to her that he did.

Max hung the garment on the back of his chair, then picked up his fork and began eating the rest of his applesauce. He looked at Caitlin with a nonchalant smile and gestured at her plate. "You don't want your food to get cold." Although that wasn't the only thing getting chilled around there, he thought as cool air rushed over him.

Caitlin took her chair at the table and picked up her sandwich. She barely suppressed a shiver at the breeze that flirted around the room, but she refused to give Max the satisfaction.

"Gee, Mom, it's cold in here, don't you think?" Jordan complained.

"Certainly not, Jordie. I find a nice, cool breeze refreshing, especially after the past few unusually warm days. Don't you, Max?" Caitlin blinked her eyes innocently in his direction.

"Oh, indeed I do," he agreed, staring her down in what had somehow become a battle of wills.

"Well, I think it's cold, Mom. Anyway, I'm finished eating," Jordan mumbled as he stuffed the last of his sandwich into his mouth. "Can I go play?"

"Hmm?" With an effort Caitlin tore her gaze from Max's. "Oh, sure, Jordie. No, wait. Maybe you'd better have your bath first. Okay?"

"Do I hafta?" At her nod, he grimaced, then brightened. "I'll take some G.I. Joe men with me." Jordan ran down the hall into the bathroom.

"Can I get you anything else?" Caitlin offered politely, looking back at Max. "Another sandwich or more applesauce?" Why didn't he put on the shirt? It was downright chilly now. She wondered sourly if it was possible to get frostbite in April.

"No, I'm fine, thanks," Max answered. For Pete's sake, would you please close that window? he silently implored. His goose bumps had goose bumps.

Caitlin stood, took her plate over to the sink, and rinsed it off. A stiff breeze billowed the yellow gingham curtains and ruffled Caitlin's hair.

When she walked back to the table to get Max's plate, she saw a sudden appreciative gleam light his eyes, and followed his intent gaze to where it rested on her chest. The cool air had caused another reaction as well. Her nipples had puckered into hard points and pressed quite obviously against her shirt. Max's gaze lingered and his hands twitched as if ready to reach out.

"Well." She whirled around and hurried over to the window. "That's enough fresh air for now, I think," she said as she closed the window, her cheeks instantly heating.

Max leaned back in the chair and stretched out his legs, lacing his fingers together behind his head. He grinned, enjoying Caitlin's discomfiture. So much for round one, he thought in devilish satisfaction.

[illegible]

[illegible] tapped on the [illegible] poked her head. "Jordan, have you finished? Did you [illegible]" [illegible]

[illegible]

Four

"Here's your shirt." The moment the dryer stopped, Caitlin jerked opened the door, grabbed Max's shirt, and thrust it at him. "Put it on before you catch cold."

"I'm perfectly comfortable," Max said complacently. "Especially now that you've closed the window."

"Put the shirt on or I'll open the window again," Caitlin said through gritted teeth as she stalked past him and went down the hall.

She tapped on the bathroom door, then poked in her head. "Jordan, have you finished? Did you use soap? Hmm. Looks dry." She paused. "Try it again, Jordie, and this time use the soap, okay?" She shook her head as she closed the bathroom door.

"Does he do that often?"

Caitlin jumped at the voice coming from just behind her and spun around.

"Are you okay?" Max asked in concern. Her face suddenly pale, she looked as if she might faint.

Caitlin took a deep breath, her hands clenching the door frame. "Oh, yes, yes, I'm fine. I just don't handle surprises very well." She managed to smile, but her voice shook a little. "To answer your first question, yes, Jordan tries to skip the soap every chance he gets. I think there's some kind of contest in first grade to see which boy can accumulate the most dirt."

"Who's winning?" Max said lightly, though his watchful eyes perused her thoughtfully.

"I don't know, but I hope it's not Jordie." Caitlin was thankful that Max had put on his shirt. "By the way, I thought I'd fix myself a cup of herb tea. Do you want one?"

"Would you happen to have any coffee on hand?"

Caitlin shook her head a little. She figured Max would be a coffee drinker. Obviously, he didn't know about all the deleterious effects caffeine had on the human body. "I'll see what I can find." With an effort she released her grip on the wooden frame and went back into the kitchen.

Max followed her and watched as she put on a pot of water to boil, then rummaged through her kitchen cabinets. So far he'd come up with two intriguing pieces to the puzzle. One, Caitlin did not like to be touched. Two, she panicked when someone came up behind her without warning. Max considered this for a moment and didn't like the picture he came up with. Had Caitlin been married to an abuser? He had never considered himself the violent sort, but he'd love to get his hands on the guy, whoever he was. Ten minutes with him, that was all he'd need to even the score. Hell, he'd take five minutes.

Caitlin couldn't help but be aware of his considering looks. As a matter of fact, she had just realized that she seemed to know *whenever* Max looked at her, as if she had built-in radar where he was concerned. She frowned at the thought as she set a steaming cup in front of him. "Um, I managed to find a jar of instant decaf. I'm not sure how old it is, but I guess that kind of coffee doesn't spoil or anything, does it?"

Max gave a weak smile and surreptitiously sniffed the brew, just to make sure it didn't smell of some unknown substance. Obviously cooking was not one of her strong points. A sudden picture of the clutter in her living room flashed through his head. Apparently, neither was housekeeping.

Just then a flesh-colored blur partially wrapped in blue terry cloth came dashing out of the bathroom, ran down the hall and up the stairs, dripping water all the way.

"Jordan?" Caitlin called after his disappearing figure. "Next time, dry yourself before you leave the bathroom." With a shrug she reached for the sponge mop and blotted up the trail of water spots. She looked up to see Max's grin.

"He's some kid, isn't he?" he commented.

"He is that," she agreed softly. "He's a real mess sometimes, and too clever for his own good, but he's the most important thing in my life."

"Does, ah, your ex-husband see Jordan very often?"

Max knew he'd broached a taboo subject when her eyes shuttered and she averted her head. He expected her to ignore his ill-timed question, but to his surprise she murmured, "I've never been married." Her voice held a slight trace of defiance, as if daring him to say anything about it.

Max fell silent. So she was an unwed mother.

The idea didn't bother him at all. In this day and age, when alternatives were so readily available, he admired that she'd chosen to keep and raise her child. "You've done a wonderful job with him," he said, mentally filing away the fact that she hadn't been married to an abusive husband.

"You really think so?" She turned to look at Max, her face earnest. "I've tried, but sometimes it's hard. I mean, with the business and all, I don't exactly run my life on a schedule or anything."

"He seems happy and healthy. He's polite, friendly, and normally rambunctious. That means he's well adjusted. Remember, I have three nephews. That qualifies me as an expert on kids."

She smiled a little. "Oh, it does, does it?"

"Just call me Dr. Spock."

Caitlin's smile widened. "Oh, do you want some more coffee?" She gestured at his nearly empty cup. "There's more in the jar."

"No, thanks anyway. I better be—"

"Mom?" Jordan called from the top of the stairs. "I'm ready to go to bed now."

"Okay, honey," Caitlin called back. "I'll be up in a minute."

"Can Max say good night too?"

She quickly looked at Max, and he nodded. "Yes, Jordie."

They went up, and Caitlin watched Max with thoughtful eyes as he sat on the edge of Jordan's bed and told Jordan a funny story with obvious relish. Maybe it was the time he spent with his three nephews, but Max acted so natural, so comfortable with Jordan and, of course, Jordan responded to this interest without reservation.

Her heart ached a little. She knew Jordan hungered for a male influence in his life. Rick had tried, whenever possible, to include Jordan in his activities with his son, like camping and backyard baseball, but it wasn't the same as having a male's undivided attention. It was no wonder he'd responded so quickly to Max.

But she worried Jordan would end up being hurt. After all, Max was going to be around for only a week or two longer. How was Jordan going to feel when Max went on to the next job? Perhaps she should stop this before it went any further. Not that she was involved with Max, but she had let him sort of barge his way in. She needed to make Max back off. She tried to ignore the twinge of pain that thought caused as she watched Max give Jordan a friendly hug.

Caitlin fell silent as she and Max went back downstairs, thoughts tumbling one after the other through her head. She had to have time to get her head together. She walked straight to the front door and opened it, letting Max know without words that he was being told to leave.

"Thank you for dinner," he said, then smiled wryly. "And thanks for the—ahem!—breath of fresh air."

An answering smile, albeit a small one, curved her lips. "I'll have the contract for you in a couple of days. It was nice of you to bring it by."

Max reached over and took Caitlin's hand. He pretended not to notice her subtle efforts to pull it away as he held it cradled between both of his. "I guess I owe you a dinner now. How about one night this week? You can bring Jordie if you like."

Caitlin felt a trembling begin deep inside when Max's thumb started tracing circles in her palm. "I, uh, dinner's not necessary."

"Oh, but it is. You fed me."

The trembling spread to her legs. "Consider it thanks for letting Jordie and his friend use your car phone."

"Letting the boys use my phone was my pleasure, so I still owe you a dinner."

"That's okay," she insisted breathlessly, trying once more to slide her hand from between his. "It was just a sandwich."

Max tightened his warm grip, both of his thumbs now massaging the sensitive inside of her wrist. "Oh, but I insist on paying you back with dinner. What night?"

Caitlin gave one more tug, and this time met with success. "Thanks anyway, Max, but no."

"How about Friday night?" He did not give up easily.

Caitlin drew in a deep breath, then let it out slowly. "I don't date." She opened the screen door. "If you come to the greenhouse tomorrow, you'd better wait until after lunch. Mornings are pretty hectic. You may want to wear jeans and a T-shirt since it's supposed to be hot again. Good night, Max." Her no-nonsense tone told him not to push his luck any further.

Max didn't often do as he was told. He slid a finger under her chin and tilted her head. "Such a stubborn chin," he murmured just before brushing his lips across hers. "But stubbornness intrigues me." He brushed another kiss across her nose. "Good night, Cait."

"Caitlin," she corrected him automatically.

"I'll see you tomorrow afternoon. Maybe we can decide where to go to dinner on Friday." He flashed a quick grin, pressed a brief kiss on her lips, and left, not giving her a chance to say anything.

Caitlin closed the door, then leaned back against it. Those kisses hadn't even lasted long enough for the fear to start, so how come they had lasted long enough for her lips to still be tingling from his touch? Every time he touched her, her body seemed to turn traitor. Her breasts swelled and ached with loneliness. Her hands seemed to move toward him as if attracted by magnets. Why? What was there about this one man that sent her hormone production into overdrive?

Caitlin continued to ponder that question as she lay in bed a couple of hours later staring at the ceiling. She felt like a child playing with matches. She knew she was going to be hurt and she was afraid, but she kept right on, fascinated by the warm, bright flame.

The next morning Caitlin decided not to go by the greenhouse right away. Instead, she went by the office supply company that Max had recommended. An hour later she left, her car loaded with almost everything Max had told her to get. She had even placed an order for letterhead stationery. After all, she'd been in business for some time now, and she felt her correspondence should look professional.

Out of curiosity she had priced a couple of the new electronic typewriters but decided that she got along just fine with her twelve-year-old electric. Actually she had an uneasy truce with it. True, the Z and the Q stuck a little, but she didn't use those letters very often anyway. She didn't want to press her luck with a fancy, expensive machine, only to find out it hated her.

By a quarter to one, Caitlin had watered the

entire greenhouse and spent two hours on the telephone. She was putting together an order of two hundred assorted potted herbs to be picked up the next day, when the sound of shoes scrunching across the gravel brought up her head. It was Max. Her heart pounded a little faster, but she decided it was because he'd startled her. She hid a smile when she noticed what he wore. If those clothes were his idea of casual, he needed lessons.

He wore dress slacks and another pristine white shirt with a maroon tie. In concession to the heat, he'd left off the jacket, but he still wore those expensive leather shoes. Maybe it was just as well he didn't show up in jeans. She had a feeling that his long legs and narrow hips outlined in tight denim would thoroughly arouse her libido.

"Hi," Caitlin said, feeling somewhat shy. "I'll be ready in a few minutes. I need to finish getting this order together."

"Can I help?" Max asked as his eyes swept over her. Jeans again. He stifled a sigh. He knew dresses wouldn't exactly be appropriate for working in a greenhouse, but he had a sudden longing to see her bare legs again. Of course, the way the snug denim hugged her firm bottom wasn't bad, and he really couldn't complain about the way the pink T-shirt clung to her breasts.

"If you want. Right now I'm picking twenty-five pots of sweet basil—that's what's on this end of the table here—and putting them into these boxes. You could turn to that table right behind you and pick twenty-five pots of garlic chives—that's the grassy-looking stuff—and put them into this box right here."

As Caitlin talked, she finished packing the basil

and moved on to English lavender. She savored the spicy scent as she began loading them.

"Now what?" Max asked when he was done with his task.

"Now I'm going to carry the boxes up to the front, by the door, so they'll be ready to be picked up first thing in the morning."

"Was that what those boxes up there were? I noticed them when I came in."

"That's right. Customers send their trucks for them. I already have a box of Italian parsley, one of sage, one of thyme, one of lemon balm. And one of tarragon. They're for The Green Unicorn. That's a retail plant shop in Richmond."

"These are all for cooking, right?"

Caitlin grinned. "No bubbling caldrons today. Sorry to disappoint you. Although parsley is a natural diuretic, and tea made from sage or thyme is supposed to help upset stomachs."

"It would give me one," Max mumbled as he followed Caitlin to the office.

When Max saw the bags of supplies on the desk, he gave a low whistle. "You actually got these."

"You said I needed them, didn't you?"

"Well, you seemed reluctant—"

"Not about average, everyday office supplies. The only thing I objected to was the computer," Caitlin reminded him.

"And that's the one thing that you could really put to good use. If you could only see what it—"

"Here, kitty, kitty," Caitlin interrupted him.

"What are you doing?"

"I'm calling Charlemagne. Now that I know he's an attack cat, I'm going to train him to get you every time you mention computers in that besotted tone of voice."

"Besotted!" Max protested. "What do you mean, besotted?"

"Just what I said. You start going on about computers in the same reverent voice that Jordan uses when he talks about his favorite baseball player."

"I do not!"

Caitlin smiled. "Oh, yes, you dooooo," she sing-songed.

"Oh, no, I dooon't," Max sang back, and took a step toward her.

"Do too!" she teased.

"Do not!" He took another step toward her.

"Too!"

"Not!" Max took one more step, then placed his hands on the desk, one on either side of her, effectively trapping her. His eyes greedily fastened on her mouth.

"I am not besotted with computers," he murmured, his warm breath fanning her cheek. "The only thing I seem to be besotted with these days is a pint-sized angel with golden curls and chocolate-brown eyes." He lowered his head and feathered soft kisses across her cheek to her mouth.

"No—" was all Caitlin got out before his lips moved over hers. As delicate as a baby's touch, as warm as a summer day, his lips seduced until hers softened in surrender.

Caitlin quivered at the hot, weak feeling that suffused her. Her hands fluttered up and lay, open-palmed, on his chest. Her mouth opened to the persistent urging of his tongue, and with a groan of triumph he moved in to explore this new territory as his arms tightened around her.

One minute she was feeling the heat of his body,

the beating of his heart. The next, her private demon infused her hands with the strength necessary to push him away.

Max stared at her for a long moment before he realized that it was terror, not passion, that glazed her eyes. Her lips had tasted so sweet, so right, and only the blind panic that flared in her unseeing gaze kept Max from pulling her back. He took a deep breath, realizing that he'd crossed some invisible barrier.

The fear on her face ate at him like acid, and he knew he had to do something to ease it. He tentatively reached out a hand and ran his fingers gently down her cheek, all the while murmuring reassurances. He wasn't even sure what he said, but it didn't seem to matter.

After a minute or two Caitlin blinked and gave a tremulous smile. "I'm sorry." Her voice was a choked whisper, and a dull flush crept up her cheeks. "I'm all right."

"You want to talk about it, Cait?" Max's voice was steady. Amazing, he thought, considering the confusion inside.

Caitlin shook her head vigorously, refusing to meet his eyes. "No."

"For God's sake! What happened to you? Who did this to you?" The words burst out before Max could stop them. A stricken look crossed her face.

"Caitlin," he began more calmly, but she whirled and ran out of the office before he could reach out a hand to her.

"You want to tell me why you're here in the middle of the day instead of at work?" Donna asked as she set iced herb tea in front of Caitlin.

Caitlin picked up her glass and took a sip. "Can't I just come visit a friend if I want?"

"You don't usually," Donna replied dryly. "Not during a business day."

"Maybe I just felt like seeing a friend today," Caitlin said defensively.

"Maybe you just needed to talk to somebody today."

Caitlin's voice was almost a whisper. "Maybe I did."

"So talk."

Silence fell for a long moment, then Caitlin said, "I'm thinking about calling Dr. Atlee."

Donna pondered this briefly. "Your therapist?"

"Yes."

"I thought you stopped seeing her several years ago because she wasn't helping."

Caitlin sighed. "I stopped seeing her because she told me I was clinging to fear because it was safer than dealing with other feelings. I didn't want to hear that. I wanted her to say some magic words and make all the fear go away."

"And now?"

"Now I think I understand what she meant. It was safer to be afraid than to risk being hurt emotionally. But I'm tired of being afraid now."

"Does this man you've met have anything to do with this decision?"

"I don't know. Maybe." Caitlin stared down at her drink as if it held the answer. "I'm not doing this because I want a relationship with him—because I don't. We're too different. But he's made me see what an emotional basket-case I've become. I'm doing this for me."

She paused for a moment, then continued. "It's like I live with a very ugly ghost. Everywhere I go, everything I do, I can see that ghost watching from the shadows, ready to pounce if I get too happy. Maybe I wasn't up to fighting that ghost several years ago, but I'm going to fight it now."

"Gonna put on the ol' boxing gloves, huh?" Donna said gently.

Caitlin smiled. "Yeah."

Donna walked over to Caitlin and gave her a hug. "Good for you. Welcome back, Caitlin dear."

Max wandered around the greenhouse. His shoes crunching in the gravel and the constant whirr of the fans were the only sounds he could hear, though he kept listening for something that would let him know Caitlin had returned. She'd been gone over an hour.

He kept replaying certain things in his mind. Caitlin did not like being touched. Caitlin got nervous when someone came up behind her. Caitlin had not been married to an abusive husband. Caitlin was afraid. Yet she was so feisty and independent, he could think of only one thing that would leave her spirit wounded in that way.

A sick feeling hit Max in the stomach and he clenched his fists so tight, his fingernails dug into his palms. She'd been raped. Maybe he was wrong, but try as he would, that seemed to be the only thing that fit. A bitter anger began to burn in Max at whoever had dared to hurt her. He could only hope the rapist had been caught and was still serving a long, long sentence. It would be safer for the bastard, he thought darkly, because God help him if he ever got his hands on him.

Max heard a footstep behind him and turned around to see Caitlin standing there.

"I wasn't sure if you'd still be here," she murmured.

"I'm not going anywhere." His words were a promise.

Caitlin looked up but did not meet his eyes, her gaze fastening on his chin instead. "Look, I'm sorry about—about what happened before. I guess I overreacted. I—"

"I understand, Cait," Max said quietly. He reached over and took her hand, holding it between his.

"Caitlin," she corrected him once more.

Max went on as if he hadn't heard. "I'd like to know what those plants are over there." He walked toward a long, low bench of seedlings in the back.

Since he still held her hand, Caitlin had no choice but to follow. As he slowly led her down the narrow aisle, he stopped at each row of seedlings and asked Caitlin what they were. Through it all, he kept a gentle but firm grip on her. Caitlin gave a few experimental tugs to free herself, but Max only tightened his fingers momentarily.

"Shouldn't we go into the office?" Caitlin asked, wondering what Max was up to.

"Hmm? Oh, no. Not yet anyway. I want to know what you use this for." He pointed to the half-bench of Scutellaria lateriflora. "Do you use this for cooking or for something else?"

Caitlin cast a puzzled glance at him. She had a feeling that he didn't really care what they were, but she answered anyway. "It's a Native American wildflower commonly called skullcap. It's a medicinal herb originally used by the American Indians. It blooms in summer with little lavender flowers at the top."

"And what's this?" He pointed to another half-bench of plants.

"Are you really interested in all this?" Caitlin asked, her voice laced with suspicion.

Max flashed an angelic smile. "Cait—"

"Caitlin," she interrupted.

"Cait, I'm interested in anything you have to say."

Caitlin snorted doubtfully. "Well then, that's Echinacea. It's also called purple coneflower. It's another native wildflower."

"What's it used for?"

"It has antiseptic qualities and is supposed to boost the immune system."

"Have you ever tried it?"

"I take some every day." Caitlin gave a quick tug to her hand.

This time Max not only tightened his grip a little but laced his fingers with hers. Caitlin frowned. "Excuse me, but could I have my hand back, please?"

"Why? Are you using it?"

"I will be."

"Well, when you're ready to use it, let me know and I'll give it back," Max said reasonably.

"Maybe I'd like to have it back now."

"But I'm getting so much use out of it now," Max said. "You wouldn't take it away just when I was getting so attached to it, would you?"

Caitlin found a smile twitching at her lips. "If you need something to hold that bad, I think Jordan has a teddy bear he could lend you." Her smile widened at the thought of Max snuggling with a teddy bear at night, then faded when the thought took one step further and had her snuggling with Max at night, their arms and legs entwined. Caitlin pressed her free hand to her stomach. What was happening to her? She'd never had fantasies like this before!

"Hey, Ms. Love, guess where I took Diana Friday night?" K.C. bounded up, then stopped short. From the look on his face it was obvious to Max that he wasn't used to coming in and finding his boss holding hands with anyone. This was something that Max dedicated himself to changing. If he had his druthers, Caitlin was going to get used to holding his hand, and often.

So far, so good, Max thought as Caitlin's hand relaxed in his and she chatted with the boy about his date and asked about Martha, who was still out with the flu. But it turned out that Max let his guard down too soon. No sooner had his grip loosened than Caitlin gave a sudden tug, freeing her hand.

Caitlin gave him a superior smile and fluttered her lashes, but Max could only grin. Slowly, he licked the end of his index finger and made an imaginary mark in the air. So much for round two, he thought. That made one for Cait. Guess they were even Steven.

Five

Caitlin didn't see Max again for two weeks. He was in northern Virginia on business, and he called every night. Each call lasted only a few minutes, but Caitlin looked forward to them anyway. She also felt a bit jealous when Jordan answered the phone and spent twenty minutes with Max, whereas when she answered, she rated only a measly ten.

On Sunday afternoon Caitlin sat on a lounge chair in the backyard and practiced the breathing relaxation exercises Dr. Atlee had told her to try. She'd seen her every day since Max went out of town. In the middle of an "inhale—count five—exhale," she heard that oh so familiar voice. "Cait?"

"Caitlin," she corrected him, then smiled up at Max. It was so good to see him, even in his dark gray three-piece suit. "Did northern Virginia finally kick you out?"

He grinned. "They said if I didn't leave, they'd shoot me on sight. May I ask what you're doing?"

Max's gaze ran over her, cataloging the details. She wore jean cutoffs that showed off her shapely legs and another T-shirt that faithfully outlined the full curves beneath, even the points of her nipples. His eyes lingered for a moment on the topknot of rebellious curls, then fastened on her warm brown eyes.

"What am I doing?" Caitlin repeated, fidgeting beneath his thorough appraisal. "I'm practicing my breathing."

"Oh, well, sure," Max murmured. "We wouldn't want to forget how to do that."

"It's a relaxation technique, Max." Caitlin sighed. "Was there a particular reason you came by?"

Max dropped down on the grass next to the chair—after spreading his handkerchief to keep his pants clean. "Yeah. I want to learn how to breathe too. Teach me, Cait."

"Caitlin."

"Hey, you call me Max, so—"

"All right then," Caitlin teased. "Maximillian."

Max gave an indignant snort. "I'll never know what my parents were thinking of when they stuck that name on me. My sister has a nice, normal name. Even my younger brother has a nice, normal name. I got stuck with Maximillian. Can you imagine the fun the other kids had with that?"

"Why didn't you go by your middle name?"

"Never." He looked horrified at the very idea.

"Why not?"

Max cast exaggerated looks over his left shoulder, then his right, as if looking for spies. In a stage whisper he said, "Cross your heart, and promise never to repeat what I am about to tell you."

Caitlin rolled her eyes and suppressed a giggle. "I promise."

"My middle name is worse than Maximillian."

"No!" Caitlin pretended to be shocked.

"Yes! It's—" He crooked his finger and motioned her closer. When she inclined her head to his, he whispered, "It's Tobias."

Her suppressed giggle finally escaped. "Tobias? Maximillian Tobias?" She flashed him an impish grin, thinking how appealing he was. "Well, since you insist on calling me Cait, I think I shall begin calling you Maximillian Tobias."

"All right, *Caitlin.* You win."

"Thank you, *Max.* I'm glad you appreciate my point of view."

"It's easy to appreciate something when you see it from the wrong end of a loaded gun," Max muttered. "Okay, Caitlin, teach me to breathe, in case I ever forget how."

Caitlin told him the basics of the exercise, but when she closed her eyes and inhaled deeply, Max found himself watching her instead of joining in. He was reminded of when his sister had been pregnant. He wondered how Caitlin would look pregnant—her breasts even lusher, her body ripe with the baby. His baby?

His fantasy extended to the making of the baby—her breasts pliant and responsive to his touch, those beautiful legs wrapped around him. The thoughts were so arousing that Max found he needed the deep breathing exercise just to regain his control.

Despite his arousal, Max couldn't help but notice that there was something different about her. He wasn't sure what. Maybe it was that her eyes had not erected their protective shield as soon as she'd seen him. Maybe it was that she had not automatically stiffened her back and squared her shoulders. Maybe it was that she seemed warmer, softer. Whatever it was, it had Max at a loss for words.

That situation was remedied quickly, however, when Jordan shot across the lawn and attacked Max, knocking him on his back. "Hi, Max. How long you been here? I thought you might call. I'm glad you came instead. When you called me, did you call from your car phone? I never got called from a car phone before." Jordan made this ninety-mile-an-hour speech as he sat on Max's chest.

Caitlin laughingly admonished him, "Jordan, you scamp, get off him right this minute. It's rude to go around squashing people."

"Can I really squash people, Mom?" Jordan asked as Max carefully sat up, brushing his shirt-sleeves clean.

"You sure can. You're quite a big boy now."

"Can I squash you, Mom?"

"Certainly—ooph!" Caitlin gasped as Jordan's arms wrapped around her and gave her a mighty squeeze. She went limp.

Max scrambled to his feet in alarm, then relaxed as Caitlin opened one eye and gave him a conspiratorial wink.

Jordan giggled. "Look, Max, I squashed her to sleep."

"So you did," Max said, settling back down on the grass. "Do you know how to wake her up?"

"Sure I do. She's real ticklish."

"She is, is she? Interesting thought," Max said suggestively, though he gave an innocent smile when Caitlin's eyes flew open.

"Hey, Mom! You're supposed to be asleep," Jordan complained.

"Oh, sorry." Caitlin closed her eyes again, but not before giving Max a warning look. She'd heard that satisfied purr in his voice.

"Patrick's here," Jordan suddenly shouted as a car horn beeped. "We're going to the park to ride the paddle boats," he said to Max. "Bye, Mom." He took off, running.

Caitlin levered herself up on her elbows and watched Jordan to make sure he got off all right. She turned back around to find Max watching her.

"Ticklish, huh?" he said.

"Not at all," she told him with a vigorous shake of her head. "Jordan was just saying that."

With a gleam in his eye Max said, "So you're saying that Jordan fibbed."

"Of course not!" Caitlin protested indignantly.

"I didn't think so." He stretched out his hands toward her ribs.

"Don't you dare!" she squealed. "Or I'll retaliate."

"That may well be the high point of my whole week," Max murmured and tickled her, grinning at her laughter.

"Vengeance is mine!" she declared with glee, and made a jab or two at Max's ribs, gratified to hear a chortle burst from his lips. Caitlin leaned forward to try again, and lost her balance, falling fully against him. The laughter died on her lips when she looked down, her face only inches from his.

Max reached up one hand and cradled her face tenderly in his palm. "I love hearing you laugh,

Caitlin," he whispered. "You have no idea how much."

Caitlin held her breath, waiting for the ugly panic to strike, only it didn't. Not even when Max's thumb ran across her bottom lip. Not even when Max urged her head down to his and brushed his lips across hers.

Not even when he slipped his tongue between her suddenly parted lips and ran the tip lightly over her teeth. And not even when his hand stroked lightly over the front of her T-shirt, causing her nipple to tighten and throb at his touch.

All too aware of the tenuousness of her compliance, Max pressed one more feather-light kiss on her lips, then drew back, searching her face. Instead of the dread he had feared to see on her face, he saw only bewilderment.

Although Caitlin felt a lot of emotions at the moment, not one of them was fear. Slowly she sat up, her eyes never leaving him. "I, ah, think I'll go fix us both a cold drink. Would you rather have herb tea, regular tea, or club soda?"

"Regular tea," Max said. "Hold the lemon." He smiled as he got to his feet, then followed her into the house. He was not at all upset with the way things had gone. Not at all.

While Caitlin prepared their drinks, Max sat at the kitchen table—after removing a large stack of newspapers from the chair. He pushed aside puzzle pieces and G.I. Joe men from the table to clear a place for the glasses. When he saw breakfast and lunch dishes piled in the sink and another large stack of newspapers on the floor next to the stove, he sighed.

"Thanks," he said when she set his tea in front of him.

"No lemon." She smiled.

"Great. Could I ask you a silly question?" he ventured as he spied yet another stack of newspapers—this one about three feet tall—in the hallway.

"Sure."

"What's with all the newspapers?"

"Oh," she answered breezily, "I just cleaned them out of the bedroom. I got tired of climbing over them to get to my bed."

"Did the thought ever occur to you that you might throw them away?"

She looked horrified. "Whatever for? I've spent months collecting these."

"Why? Is some organization having a paper drive?"

"Well, no, but someone might, and then I'd be ready for them. It's recycling, you know."

"You mean you're collecting these just *in case*?" Max asked, incredulous.

Caitlin sat up a little straighter and stuck out her chin. "You have something against recycling?"

"Nothing. Nothing at all," he hastened to assure her. "It's just that it might make things, well, a little less cluttered if you put them, say, outside in the garage."

Caitlin stiffened slightly. Cluttered, huh? "I can't do that," she said a tad too sweetly. "That's where I keep my aluminum cans."

"Perhaps if you—"

Caitlin stood abruptly, almost knocking over her chair. "If you don't like my housekeeping methods, Mr. Shore, feel free to leave. I may be too messy for your impeccable taste, but I don't think I'm in danger of being closed down by the Board of

Health. At least not yet." Head high, back stiff, she marched into the living room.

Max hurriedly got to his feet and followed her, tripping over yet another stack of papers. He put out his hands to brace himself as he fell, catching the edge of a small parson's table covered with a collection of plants in little ceramic pots. The table teetered, and the plants slid off directly onto Max's path.

A horrified no barely escaped Caitlin's lips before Max landed, hands first, on the ceramic shards.

She stumbled across the room and knelt beside him as he sat up. "Heavens, Max, are you all right?"

"I'm just fine," he said dryly, glancing down at his hands. "If you don't mind blood."

"Goodness! You'd better come into the bathroom so we can get you cleaned up and find out what that cut really looks like." Her heart sank as she said it. There seemed to be a lot of blood.

To her relief, most of the cuts were superficial—treatable with antiseptic cream and bandages. But one deep gash on his left palm continued to ooze blood ten minutes later. Worried, Caitlin insisted on driving Max to the hospital to have it stitched.

She waited anxiously in the emergency room. Finally, the same nurse who had taken him into the treatment room came out. Caitlin stood. "Is he ready to go now?"

"It's going to take a bit longer than we expected," the nurse explained. "He fainted."

Caitlin gasped. "From loss of blood?" She didn't think he'd bled that much.

"Not exactly," the nurse hedged. "Look, he

might not like it that I told you this, but when the doctor took out the hypodermic to give him his tetanus shot, Mr. Shore took one look at it and keeled over."

Caitlin bit back a smile. The image of the ever-so-self-assured Maximillian Shore fainting at the sight of a needle infused her with amusement, and with a sudden tenderness as well.

"You can go on back and see him if you like," the nurse offered. "Examining room three."

"No," Caitlin murmured. "Thanks anyway. He might not want me to know he fainted. I'll just wait here." She sat down, still smiling, and picked up a magazine.

It was another half hour before Max finally came out, his hand bandaged in white gauze. "Hi," he said, wagging his fingers at her.

"Hi, yourself." Caitlin set the magazine down on the table and stood. "Gee," she exclaimed innocently, "how many stitches did you have to get? Must have been a lot, hmm? You sure were in there a long time."

Max ran a finger around his collar and winced. "Um, a few," he finally said noncommittally.

Caitlin looked at him, wide-eyed.

"You know," he accused her.

"Know what?" she said, then smiled. "C'mon, tough guy." She grabbed her purse, hooked her arm through his, and walked out to the parking lot. "Why don't we go back by my house and I'll fix you supper before I take you home?"

"You don't have to take me home. I can drive."

"Not with that hand, you can't," she said firmly.

Max didn't say anything for a moment, but his mind was racing ahead. As much as he hated being without his car, he could use this situation to get Caitlin to spend a little more time with him. He just wouldn't mention that his sister lived three blocks away from his house. "Well," he finally said, "maybe you're right. But how am I going to get to work in the morning?" He waited expectantly for her answer.

"I guess I can come by and pick you up on my way to the greenhouse in the morning. I don't open the doors there until nine anyway. You probably get to work earlier than that, don't you?"

"I'm usually there by eight or eight-thirty."

"Well, you see? It'll work out perfectly."

Perfectly, Max thought. He'd gotten her to offer to take him to work. Now, if he could just get her to take him home too. "I really hate to ask you this, but could you pick me up from work? I'll have to get my car from you."

"Oh, I hadn't thought of that." Caitlin paused, her mind racing through the list of errands she'd planned on taking care of the following evening. "I guess I could. What time do you usually leave?"

"Five-thirty or six. I'm the boss." He grinned. "I can leave anytime I want to, so if that's not convenient—"

"Oh, it's fine." Caitlin gave a mental shrug. "I usually close up the greenhouse around five, so that will give me time to pick up Jordie from the sitter."

The drive to Caitlin's house was quiet with both Caitlin and Max immersed in their own thoughts. Caitlin wondered how she could arrange her day so that she could pick Max up at five-thirty and still have time to drop next month's flyer by the printers, pick up her order at the department store, drop off an overdue library book, and do the grocery shopping.

Max, on the other hand, toyed with several ways to get Caitlin to agree to dinner on Monday night. He'd gotten her to say she'd take him to work and even to pick him up. It should be simple enough, he decided, to get her to go out to dinner, if he handled it tactfully enough.

Back at home, Caitlin was brisk and efficient as she threw together a light supper. She set filled plates on the table and Max stared at his, trying to identify the strange lumps in the white sauce over green noodles.

Obviously he had a question mark in his eyes when he glanced up at Caitlin, because she casually said, "Creamed tofu on spinach noodles. It's my own recipe. Fresh garlic for flavor, roasted sunflower seeds for crunch. Jordie calls it Tofu Surprise because sometimes I add onion or mushrooms or sprouts. It's very flexible."

"Right." Max frowned, then decided to try it. After all, it couldn't be as bad as the Unidentified Fried Object he'd had last week. Then again, it could be worse since it had tofu. He always walked past the soy bean curd stuff at the supermarket. It sounded disgusting. Let's hope it doesn't taste as bad, he thought as he bravely lifted his fork.

Surprise. It didn't taste disgusting. But it didn't taste great either. As a matter of fact, Max found it almost completely tasteless except for the garlic. He muffled a sigh and took another bite. The things he would do just to have a few more minutes with her. He fortified himself with the knowledge that he could always call Piggy's Pizza when he got home. They delivered.

Halfway through the meal Jordan came bounding in, full of his customary endless energy. As he talked nonstop about his day, Caitlin shook her head a little and smiled. Oh, to be so young and so full of verve. Sometimes she felt tired just watching him. "Hey, fella," she broke in with a smile. "It might do you some good to slow down enough to take a breath, don't you think?"

"Aw, Mom." Jordan didn't even miss a beat. "Anyway, Max, what we did was so neat. We took the wheels off his skateboard and fastened them on this board. And then we took a coffee can and—I know. C'mon, Max, I'll show ya. I got pencils and paper and stuff in my room." With that Jordie took Max by the hand and tugged him upstairs.

"Hey, Max," Caitlin called after them. "Do you want me to save the rest of your supper?"

Save it? he thought. Heaven help him! "Ah, no," he replied. "Thanks anyway, but I'm full."

"But you hardly ate half. Jordie, let Mr. Shore finish his dinner first, okay?"

"That's not necessary," Max said quickly. "I'd really like to see what Jordan spent his day building."

"Well, if you're sure . . ."

"Oh, I'm sure." *I'm sure my taste buds will never be the same, that's what I'm sure of,* he thought.

"I'll wrap the rest of this and you can take it home."

"Gee, thanks," he said. Maybe Cholly, his golden Lab, would eat it.

"Don't worry, Max," Jordan said in a conspiratorial whisper as he stopped on the stairs. "Mom doesn't always put tofu in everything."

"That's good to know."

"And it's really okay sometimes. Specially when she squishes it up with honey and cinnamon and puts it on toast. What'd you do to your hand? Did you have to have stitches? I did once. Three stitches in my knee and . . ." Jordan continued to chatter on as they made their way to his room.

Caitlin smiled to herself as she scraped Max's leftovers into a small container. She didn't expect him to eat it, it would probably find its way into the trash. But it would be fun watching him pretend to be delighted when she handed him the container to take home.

Caitlin stacked the dirty dishes in the sink, then decided to take advantage of the few minutes of quiet to practice her breathing exercises again, along with what Dr. Atlee called creative visualization. Caitlin settled back in a chair and closed her eyes, taking deep breaths. But after a few minutes she opened her eyes and changed positions. There, that was better. She closed her eyes and started all over again.

"Well, shoot," she murmured, and squirmed around in the chair. It wasn't working as it was supposed to. She was supposed to be visualizing herself living a completely normal and happy life. What she saw, however, was herself living a completely normal and happy life with Max. "Okay," Caitlin said to herself. "Let's try this one more time."

She twisted and turned until she felt comfortable and tried again, but no sooner had her eyes fluttered closed than she heard Max's hearty laughter.

With a good-natured sigh she got to her feet and headed upstairs. She told herself it was curiosity, but deep in her heart she admitted that some nearly frozen core in her wanted to be closer to the warmth of that laughter.

She stood in the doorway to Jordan's room for a

long time and watched them. Their heads were bent over something on Jordan's small desk and Caitlin compared the two—Max's conservatively cut brown hair next to Jordan's riot of tangled gold curls. They couldn't have been more opposite. Or looked more right together.

An impossible dream, Caitlin thought wistfully.

She hated to break up a moment that could have come straight out of a Norman Rockwell painting, but in Jordan's best interest, Max had to leave. Jordan wanted a father so much and he'd taken so quickly to Max that Caitlin knew he was beginning to cast Max in the role. It would be best if Jordan and Max didn't spent so much time together.

She tapped on the open door and said with a forced smile, "Sorry to break up the party, guys, but it's time to leave."

"Leave, Mom?" Jordan asked plaintively.

"Leave, sweetie. We have to take Mr. Shore home now. He can't drive because of his hand."

"Aw, Mom, can't he stay a little while longer?"

"Sorry, kiddo, but it's a school night. Remember?"

Max stood gracefully and ruffled Jordan's hair with his good hand, then placed it casually on the boy's shoulder. "It's okay, Jordan. We'll do this again. Come on."

Caitlin noticed the easy camaraderie between the two and felt a glimmer of discomfort at the pain it was going to cause Jordie to have his contact with Max restricted. It had to be done though. To put it off would only make things worse. She'd have a talk with Max when she picked him up in the morning and try to explain her position. Heaven only knew what she was going to say. She certainly didn't.

The ride to Max's was a quiet one. Jordan was already beginning to nod off and Caitlin seemed wrapped up in thought. Max kept a speculative eye on her as she drove, wondering what had put that pensive look on her face. He made a few attempts at conversation, but all he got from Caitlin was single-syllable responses.

He gave up in frustration. Fortunately for his temper, the drive was a short one.

Caitlin wasn't surprised at Max's house. The turn-of-the-century brownstone with its prim elegance seemed to fit him. Even the row of red geraniums highlighted by the porch light fit his traditional, conservative image. It was vastly different from her small Cape Cod with its huge windows and skylights and the garden that could best be described as a patchwork quilt. She stifled a sigh. "Good night, Max."

"Why don't you come in for a moment?"

"Thanks anyway, but I need to get Jordan home to bed. I'll be by in the morning."

"Max?" Jordan's sleepy voice came from the backseat.

"Yeah, sport."

Jordan sat up straight and looked out the window with interest as he rubbed one eye. "This where you live?"

"Sure is." Max cast an almost defiant glance at Caitlin when he asked, "Would you like to see it?"

"Sure!"

"Ah, Jordie, it's almost your bedtime and you've had a busy day," Caitlin interjected, her eyes shooting daggers at Max.

"Aw, Mom, can't we stay for just a minute? Please?"

She was going to get Max for this. She didn't know how or when, but she was definitely going to get him. "For just a minute," she conceded with another glance at Max.

"Great," Max said with an innocent smile, and led the way into his house.

Caitlin looked around while Jordan knelt on the impeccably vacuumed floor and petted the abnormally well-behaved dog. Caitlin thought dogs should be well-behaved, of course, but a dog that neither barked when you opened the door nor tried to climb up and lick your face wasn't quite normal to her way of thinking.

The interior of the house wasn't quite right either. It didn't surprise her to find it spotlessly clean and furnished tastefully, but it was bland. There were no potted plants, no brightly colored throw pillows, no magazines on the coffee table, not even the remnants of a doggie bone or rubber ball for the dog.

The worst things about it were the heavy drapes that shrouded each small window. Feeling closed in, Caitlin shuddered; then, as she was also polite, she said, "It's very nice, Max. Come on, Jordie. Time to go."

Jordan grumbled a little, but gave Max a hug, then walked with Caitlin out to the van. When Caitlin had buckled Jordan in, he pointed to the wrapped container on the backseat. "Max forgot his dinner, Mom."

"So he did," Caitlin murmured. On purpose, she figured, then gave a wicked smile. The least she could do was to give it to him.

Max's smiled when he opened the door to allow

Caitlin in was genuine, then became a bit forced when his gaze fell on the container. "Gee, thanks," he said, then rested his eyes on Caitlin's lips. "I have something for you too, something I've waited all evening to give to you, so I'm especially glad you came back."

"Oh?" Not a particularly brilliant statement, but it was the best Caitlin could come up with on the spur of the moment. She could almost feel his gaze as she backed away.

Max took a step forward. "Yes," he said, his breath warm against her cheek. "What I have for you is—" His voice died as his lips met hers in a kiss that teased and coaxed and lured. He brought up one hand to cradle her face but didn't pull her into his arms, although he ached to. Instead, he was gentle, one hand caressing her hair, the other resting at her waist.

Only when her lips softened and parted beneath his did Max deepen the kiss, still keeping a tight rein on his self-control, though his heart pounded and his hands shook with the effort. His seeking tongue made tentative forays into the honeyed interior of her mouth, and she met the gentle thrusts of his tongue with her own.

When her hands came up to his shoulders and flattened, as if to push him away, Max tensed with anticipated rejection. Instead, her hands slid over his shoulders to his back, leaving Max choked with wonder. He pressed sweet, urgent kisses over her cheek to her ear, then lifted her onto her tiptoes and pressed a single warm kiss in the hollow of her throat before releasing her.

"Good night, Caitie." His voice was the barest of whispers as he opened the front door for her.

"Good night," Caitlin murmured, one hand going to her mouth as if to assure herself that it had really happened.

"Sweet dreams, Caitie."

"Same to you, Maximillian." She flashed a sudden smile and left.

Max watched out the door long after Caitlin had driven off, his lips curved into a smile. She'd kissed him back. She'd really kissed him back.

Six

By the next morning Caitlin had convinced herself that she responded to Max because the therapy was working and she was ready to respond to any normal, attractive male. It had absolutely nothing to do with Max's particular charm or the unusual magnetic pull he seemed to exert over her. Or his clean, spicy fragrance, or the devastatingly right way his lips felt.

Her heartbeat accelerated and her breath quickened as she drove to his house to pick him up for work. Max didn't help matters, either, by jumping into the front seat and immediately tugging Caitlin to him for a brief but thorough kiss. "'Morning, Cait."

"Caitlin." She corrected him without thinking and hurriedly started the van again. She applied the gas, and the motor hummed, but the van wouldn't move. She tried it again, and the engine raced, but the van still didn't move. She glanced at Max before shrugging apologetically. "I—it must be stuck or something."

"Well," Max said, biting back a smile, "it might help if you put the van into reverse instead of park."

Her cheeks flaming, she gritted her teeth as she shifted gears. Honestly, he was the most provoking man! Good thing the ride to Max's office was a brief one, she thought, and Max didn't seem to be in a talkative mood. She doubted she could string two intelligent words together. She couldn't understand why Max just smiled and whistled softly to himself the whole way.

When she pulled in front of his building, he cheerfully said, "See you at five-thirty," and pressed a brief but warm kiss on her mouth.

"Max, would you behave?" she told him. "You've got to stop doing that!"

"Doing what?" he asked with an all-too-innocent smile.

"That! As if you—as if I—" She floundered to an uncomfortable halt.

"As if you belonged to me?" He flashed a cheeky grin and shook his head. "Sorry, sweet Caitie. You'd better get used to it." Yeah, he thought, the way he was getting used to seeing the sun fight its way out of the confused tangle of curls that haloed her face. The way he was getting used to that impish way she smiled as if she'd just thought of some private joke. The way he was even getting used to the way she challenged him.

"Have a nice day, Cait."

She waited until he'd opened the door and stepped out before replying loudly, "I intend to, Maximillian Tobias."

"Touché, Caitlin," he said as she waved a hand and pulled off.

• • •

As Caitlin fought the evening rush hour traffic to pick up Max, she mentally replayed her day. Martha was back at work, so Caitlin no longer had to close the greenhouse for her morning sessions with Dr. Atlee. Today had been the best one yet, Caitlin thought. The doctor had told Caitlin how pleased she was with her progress and suggested she cut the therapy sessions to one a week and enter a women's support group. She also suggested that Caitlin was ready to take the next step toward a relationship.

Caitlin couldn't prevent the way her mind immediately leapt to Max when Dr. Atlee said that. Just as quickly, she vetoed the idea. Maybe she *was* ready for a relationship, but not with Max. They were just too different. A relationship between them would never last. Relationships with men like Max never lasted.

With a twinge of guilt she glanced at Jordie. They were nearing Max's office, and her son was already looking eagerly out the window for any sign of Max. She hoped Jordie would understand why she couldn't see Max anymore. He already thought far too much of Max for Caitlin's peace of mind.

She saw Max waiting on the corner of his street and pulled to a stop. He hopped right in, but not before a car behind them blasted its horn. "Oh, sit on it," Max muttered, then glanced down at Jordan. "Oops! Sorry."

"Oh, that's okay," Jordan said. "Mom usually says something about sunshine."

"Sunshine?" Max asked.

"Yeah. About somewhere it doesn't shine."

"Jordie!" Caitlin protested, though she found herself smiling back at Max's sudden grin. "Sometimes I forget he soaks up everything he sees and hears."

"Yeah, I know," Max said companionably, and began telling her about the time he'd tried to build a birdhouse with his nephews. Every time he'd hit his thumb with the hammer, he had immeasurably enriched their vocabulary. Of course, his sister hadn't seen it that way and he'd had a long talk with the boys about why grown-ups can say certain things and kids can't. Max found himself embellishing the story as he went, but he couldn't help it. He loved to hear Caitlin laugh unreservedly.

Seeing her eyes flash with amusement and her hair tangle around her face made Max more determined than ever to be the man to keep the laughter in her eyes. First, he had to get her to go out with him. He'd do anything to accomplish this goal, even turn Jordan into an unwitting ally, if necessary.

To that end, Max cast a cautious glance at Caitlin and said, "I know a great pizza place that's right on the way home. How about if we stop there? My treat?"

"Terrific!" Jordan exclaimed. "Can we, Mom? Please?"

Caitlin shot a look at Max that told him she knew exactly what he had done and that he could expect to hear further on the subject. However, in front of Jordan she had no choice but to give in gracefully, if reluctantly.

As they pulled into the parking lot of Piggy's Pizza, Max allowed himself one brief, self-satisfied smile which he kept carefully hidden from Caitlin.

Okay, so his tactic was sneaky and underhanded, but all was fair in love and war. He wasn't exactly sure which one this was. He didn't even know if it mattered. He could spend his life warring to make love with her or loving to make war with her.

After they took their seats and Max had placed the order, he noticed Caitlin giving a long-suffering sigh and pursing her lips. "Is, ah, something wrong, Cait?" He figured she wouldn't let him have it too bad in a public place.

Caitlin studied her fingernails a moment before glancing up. "Whatever makes you say that?" she asked dryly.

"Gee, I don't know. Maybe I'm psychic. You want to tell me or make me guess?"

"You ordered two pepperoni pizzas, Max," she said.

Since they'd eaten a few meals together, he knew what she was getting at and was ready for her. "Pepperoni pizza is good for you since it has ingredients from four basic food groups." Holding up one finger at a time, he continued. "There's meat, vegetable—that's the tomato sauce—dairy product—the mozzarella, of course—and grain, which in this case is whole wheat, as in whole wheat crust. Now you tell me if that's not healthy."

"Right," Caitlin murmured. "The tomato sauce probably has artificial flavors and preservatives, and the *whole milk* mozzarella is loaded with cholesterol. As for the pepperoni, I don't eat meat."

"Not even one or two little innocent pepperonis?"

Caitlin looked horrified. "Max, do you realize how many calories are in those little innocent things, not to mention nitrates, preservatives, and cholesterol? And the cuts of meat they use—"

Max held up a hand. "Enough. I don't really want to know where pepperoni comes from. But I do want to know if Jordan can't have any."

Caitlin glanced at her son playing a video game at the front of the restaurant. "I don't force Jordie to be a vegetarian just because I am. When he buys lunch at school or goes to a friend's house, he can eat whatever he wants. I simply choose not to cook meat at home."

"So what does Jordan usually choose to eat on his own?" Max asked with interest.

Caitlin smiled a little. "Except for spaghetti day at school, he usually asks me to pack his lunch."

"What does he do at a friend's house?"

Her smile widened. "The little sneak decides whether or not he's a vegetarian based on how well he likes what's been fixed for dinner."

Max laughed, then excused himself, saying Jordan probably needed another quarter for the game by now.

When he returned several minutes later, Caitlin raised her eyebrows. "Heavens, Max, just how many quarters did you give Jordie anyway?"

"Just a couple," Max replied easily. "It took so long because I had to get exact change from the cashier."

The real reason it had taken so long became apparent a few minutes later when the waitress brought their order. Instead of *two* pepperoni pizzas, only one was pepperoni; the other was what the waitress called a "Piggy's Garden minus the pig."

"That's sausage, mushrooms, green peppers,

onions, shredded carrots, and sliced tomatoes minus the sausage," Max explained.

Goodness, but he confused her, Caitlin thought as she chewed on a bite of her pizza. First he'd do something that aggravated her, then he'd turn around and do something sweet. That really took the wind out of her sails. He wouldn't even let her stay mad at him.

When Caitlin pulled into Max's driveway, it was still fairly early. Max got Caitlin inside by mentioning that he'd just bought a computer game for his nephews to use. Would Jordan like to see it?

Max nearly winced at Caitlin's razor-sharp glare but instead smiled and seated her on the sofa. After taking Jordan upstairs and settling him at the computer, he returned to Caitlin. When she took a deep breath and opened her mouth, obviously with the intention of speaking her mind, Max escaped to the kitchen to fix her a drink.

"Here you go," he said a few minutes later when he came back and handed her a glass of orange juice. "No lemon."

Ignoring the lemon joke, she immediately set the drink on the table. "Max, I will not—"

"I'd better go upstairs and make sure Jordan's doing okay." Max hurriedly got to his feet and went off, leaving Caitlin's mouth hanging open in midsentence.

She turned her perplexed gaze to the dog sitting politely at her feet, waiting for her to notice him. While she scratched him behind the ears, she proceeded to tell the dog exactly what she thought of one Maximillian Tobias Shore.

Max, coming back, heard what she was saying and deciding discretion was the better part of valor, turned around to join Jordan for a few more minutes. He knew he wouldn't get away with it when he stepped on the one squeaky spot on the whole staircase.

Caitlin turned her head with a snap and fastened her eyes on Max. "Oh, no, you don't, you sneaky rat! Get over here and sit down. I want to talk to you. Now!" With her arms crossed and her back straight, she waited while Max descended. When he sat right next to her on the sofa, it disconcerted her, but she refused to give him the satisfaction of moving away.

"You wanted to see me, sweet Caitie?" he asked.

"You bet your stitches, I do," she retorted in a low but heated voice. "What on earth do you mean by using Jordie like that?"

"Like what?"

"Don't play dumb with me, Max Shore. You used him to get your way tonight. Don't you dare deny it!" She turned her head away so he wouldn't see that she really wasn't as mad as she hoped she sounded.

"Okay, I won't," Max said, unruffled. "I used him to keep you from pushing me away."

"Pushing you away?" Caitlin turned back to look at him.

"Don't play dumb with me, Caitlin Love. You've been planning to push me away. Don't you dare deny it." He tossed her words back at her. "But I'm not going to let it happen. We've got too much going for us."

"Like what?"

Max slid a finger under her chin and lifted her

face to his. "Like this," he said, and brushed a butterfly-delicate kiss across her left eyelid.

"Max," she protested softly.

He ignored the protest and kissed her other eyelid. "And like this." His lips teased one corner of her mouth, then the other, and trailed to her ear and the hollow beneath it.

"Max," she protested more feebly than before.

"And this," he breathed against the soft skin of her neck and traced a path with his tongue down to the collar of her blouse.

"Max." Her voice was the barest whisper, all traces of protest gone now. She wanted more. The only parts of him touching her were the finger under her chin and his lips. And she wanted more. Her hands came up and fastened onto his shoulders.

Max lifted his head just enough to see Caitlin's eyes. Fear wasn't there, only a shy expectancy. His gut twisted and he swallowed, resting his hands lightly at her waist, trying to dampen the passion that threatened to blaze out of control. He couldn't take a chance on coming on too strong and scaring her away.

Only when he had regained a fragment of his self-control did he allow himself to sip at her lips again and again, light kisses that seduced and tempted. It wasn't until he felt her fingers curl into his back that he deepened the kiss. His tongue made daring forays into her mouth, luring hers to follow. When it did, he finally allowed his fingers the luxury of slowly sliding upward, to just beneath her full breasts.

Her whole body felt liquid and effervescent, as if afloat in a frothy sea, she thought hazily, and tightened her hands on his shoulders. He was her anchor, her security.

The feeling of security crumbled, however, when Max's large, warm hands moved up to cover her breasts. Panic loomed its ugly head and Caitlin stiffened as her breath caught in her throat.

Max felt the change in her and ordered tenderly, "Open your eyes, sweet Caitie. Look at me." When she did so, he held her gaze with his. "Just keep looking at me," he whispered. "You're so beautiful, so warm, so soft." He continued to murmur soothing words as his hands moved gently over her full breasts.

Caitlin's breath caught again, only this time she knew it had nothing to do with old specters and everything to do with the vibrant, sensual man who held her in his arms. She tilted her head back and closed her eyes, inviting him to take her lips again.

Max accepted the invitation gladly. Caitlin, vibrant and sassy, was enchanting, but Caitlin, soft and flushing, took his breath away. Only the knowledge that there was a small boy upstairs kept Max from going further. He regretfully slid his hands down to a safer perch at her waist and pressed one last kiss to her lips.

"God, you are so sweet," he murmured in her ear, then pulled back just enough to look at her. "Now tell me you don't date," he demanded.

She opened her eyes and returned his gaze. His eyes—were they royal blue? Midnight blue? Her lashes fluttered down. "I don't," she said in answer to his question. When his lips swooped down to nibble the side of her neck, she said breathlessly, "I—ah—I could make an exception."

"You do that," he growled against her neck. "For this Friday night."

"Um, I—I don't know if I can find a sitter for Jordie on such short notice," Caitlin hedged.

Max sharply nipped the base of her throat, then soothed it with his tongue. "Friday night. I'll pick you up at seven-thirty."

Go on, insisted a little voice inside her. What harm could it do? They were very different, that's true, but accepting a dinner invitation certainly wasn't saying yes to a proposal of marriage. Besides, the warm, liquid feeling in her limbs was nice, more than nice. Wonderful. She owed it to herself to explore this feeling further. "Okay. I'll try to work something out," she acquiesced breathlessly as Max's lips continued their delicate assault on her throat.

"Mom? Is Max kissing it better or is this just some mushy stuff?" an interested voice piped from the stairs.

Caitlin could feel hot color paint her cheeks and was speechless, but Max, unembarrassed, looked up and said, "What do you think, Jordie?"

"Who knows?" Jordan gave an unconcerned shrug. "Do you have anything to eat?"

"Jordie!" Caitlin admonished, hoping she wasn't as red as she felt. "We ate just a little while ago."

"It was hours ago, Mom, and I'm starvin'."

"Growing boy, Mom," Max said. "Is it okay if I give him a piece of fruit?"

Jordan didn't wait for his mother to answer. "Do you have any bananas? I love bananas."

"Well, bananas it is, then. Okay?" He waited for Caitlin's nod before heading Jordan toward the kitchen.

Caitlin got to her feet and wandered around the living room, looking for signs that might reveal something else about the man who lived here. The furniture was nice but nondescript, and, although Caitlin was no expert, not terribly expensive.

The one piece that didn't fit was an antique rolltop desk in perfect condition. There were intricate carved designs on the side panels and the wood gleamed with the patina of fine old cherry. Even the brass fittings had been polished till they shone. She ran a hand carefully across the surface.

"It's beautiful, isn't it?"

Caitlin turned at the sound of Max's voice and nodded. "Oh, yes."

"I found it a few years ago at a flea market in Vermont. It's probably about a hundred and fifty years old. It was one of the few things I managed to keep."

"Managed to keep?"

"After the divorce. Jackie hired some hotshot attorney, and I had a kid fresh out of law school. I'm still not quite sure how she managed it, but she got just about everything. I fought tooth and nail to keep the desk and the business. In the end, that was about all I kept," Max said matter-of-factly, as if it didn't matter.

Did it really not matter, Caitlin wondered, or was Max a good enough actor to make it seem that way? Did anyone emerge from a failed marriage unscathed? "How long were you married?" Caitlin asked quietly.

"Three years. Three of the longest years of my life."

"Why—no, never mind. It's none of my business." Caitlin dropped her gaze back to the desk.

"It's more your business than you're willing to admit. Ask me anything."

"Okay." She glanced up. "What happened?" Caitlin couldn't believe she'd really asked such a nosy question. She also couldn't believe how interested she was in the answer.

Max leaned against the desk. "I met Jackie when I did some work for her father's company. Her father was impressed with me and promised I'd really go places. He began to invite me to various functions. I'd usually end up as Jackie's date. It really didn't seem like much of a hardship. Jackie is well educated and beautiful."

Caitlin swallowed back a twinge that might have been jealousy and nodded.

Max sighed. "Somehow, we wound up engaged. That really didn't bother me too much either. I was twenty-five at the time and had been thinking about settling down. I felt I could do a lot worse." Max gave a short laugh. "Let's face it. Feeling you could do a lot worse isn't much of a reason to get married, but I was intent on making it work."

He smiled grimly. "While I was intent on making our marriage work, Jackie was intent on making *me* work. We'd been married about two years when I realized what was wrong. I wasn't rising fast enough or high enough to support Jackie in the style to which she wanted to become accustomed. She began pushing, wanting me to take advantage of her father's connections, expand my company, open branches."

"What did you do?"

"I tried to make her understand that wasn't the vision I had for my company. I didn't care about expanding. I didn't care about being the biggest, just the best. Needless to say, that didn't go over well. The first six months of the third year, we argued constantly. The last six months, we didn't speak at all. Then one day I came home and found her in bed with her father's administrative assistant. A real up-and-comer, she assured me," Max said wryly. "It was almost a relief. Until I heard what she was asking for in the divorce settlement."

"What was she asking for?"

"Everything. The house, the car, the bank accounts, the business. Even my dog. And he is *my* dog," Max exclaimed indignantly. "I've had him since I was twenty-two and right out of college. She just wanted him to spite me, I guess."

"Oh, Max, I'm so sorry."

"Don't apologize, Cait. I managed to keep the things that really mattered—the dog, the business, the desk. I probably would have kept more had I fought hard enough, but it wasn't worth the effort. I wanted to put all the ugliness behind me and get on with a new life."

"Well, it looks like you've done well with that."

Max smiled. "Yeah. And I've done even better the past few weeks. I took on this new account, you see, and met this absolute angel. I'm really hoping that one day she'll trust me enough to tell me her life story, just like I told her mine." His gaze flowed over her, lingering on kiss-swollen lips.

Caitlin whirled away. "I'd better round up Jordie. I need to get him home so he can get his homework done. At least I think he has homework. He usually does. I just don't—" Her voice died abruptly when Max reached out one hand and encircled her wrist.

"I'll let you run away this time, Caitie, but not forever."

"Don't push, Max, please." Her eyes pleaded with him.

"You've got to tell me sometime," he said softly. "You know that, don't you?"

Caitlin took a deep breath, then nodded. "Sometime. But not now."

"When?"

"When I can talk about it," she said softly.

"Mom? Can I have another banana?"

Caitlin tore her gaze away. "Absolutely not, young man. It's time for us to go home. It's only an hour till your bedtime, and you have homework to do."

"I don't have any homework tonight, Mom."

"Well, then you have spelling words you can study."

"But Mom—"

"Jordan." She said it quietly, but in the tone of voice Jordan had heard often enough to know what it meant.

Max swept Jordan up into a bear hug. "That's right, Jordan. Go on and study those spelling words. I can't have my best buddy flunk spelling."

Jordan's eyes lit up. "Am I your best buddy, Max?"

Max gave him another squeeze. It felt so good to have this young boy's trusting arms hug him back. "You bet." He set Jordan down on his feet. "You run along to the van and get the best seat. I'll send Mom out in a minute."

"Um, I've got to go, Max," Caitlin said immediately. "Thanks for the pizza."

Max's eyes gleamed. "Gee, seems I need to teach you how to say thank-you properly."

Caitlin's eyes darted to the door, then back to Max's face. She stood on tiptoe and pressed a brief kiss on his cheek. "Thank you, Max," she said demurely, and headed toward the door.

She felt hands fasten gently but firmly on her shoulders and turn her around. "Wrong again, sweet Caitie."

She smiled—a nervous smile, a shy smile—as his gaze dropped to her lips. He lowered his head to taste that smile, and felt her tremble against him. He pulled back to see her face, and what he found there reassured him that she hadn't been shaking from fear.

"Max?" Her voice was a plea and he answered by again claiming her lips. When Caitlin voluntarily parted her lips, inviting him to enter, he felt breathless, but that didn't stop him from storming in and claiming the territory for his own.

When he finally pulled away, his conquest complete, he was satisfied to see the soft, dazed look on her face. "Can you pick me up in the morning? You still have my car, you know." Max was vaguely surprised at the warm huskiness of his voice.

Caitlin nodded. "Um, why don't I pick you up a half hour early and take you back to get it? Or I could take you with me now."

A few more minutes with her. Max accepted immediately.

When they arrived at her house, Jordan bounded out and up the sidewalk with Caitlin's key in his hand. He loved to unlock the door. Max turned toward Caitlin and reached out a hand to cup her cheek. "Thanks for the rides, Cait."

"You're welcome. I'd better go in. Jordan's waiting at the door. Good night, Max."

When his head moved toward hers, she opened the van door and got out. She needed time to sort out the strange new feelings inside her, and his kisses muddled her thinking.

Max just gave an understanding smile. He was satisfied with the evening. More than satisfied. And, after all, there was always Friday night.

Seven

Caitlin's upcoming date with Max occupied her thoughts most of the week. Every day when she awoke, she lay in bed, staring at the dust motes dancing in the early morning sunlight and asked herself if she was crazy. After all, she didn't date.

She tried to convince herself that it wasn't really a date—it was simply a business dinner. However, she knew in her heart that the only business they'd discuss had nothing to do with work and everything to do with the way their bodies felt when they were together.

Friday morning she woke up earlier than usual and mentally ran through a dozen excuses for calling Max and canceling their date.

"Gee, I'm sorry, Max, but I have a mountain of purchase orders." No, that wouldn't work. Max knew exactly what the status of her paperwork was. "I have an awful headache and . . ." He wouldn't buy that either. Too trite. "I simply have to wash my hair." Ha! "I forgot that I promised Jordie I'd take him camping this weekend." Better not. She wouldn't put it past Max to invite himself along.

She was still mulling over various excuses as she dropped Jordan at school and drove to work. She even practiced a few of them out loud as she struggled with that stubborn greenhouse door she'd been meaning to get repaired.

She forgot all about her date, however, when she opened the door and Charlemagne greeted her. Meowing raucously, he wrapped himself around her ankles. When she bent down to pet him, he leapt into her arms and clung, his claws hooking firmly through the cotton of her shirt-sleeve and into her flesh.

"Ouch!" She pried his claws loose, then laid a soothing hand on his head. "What's the matter, baby? What's got you spooked?" Curious, she looked around but noticed nothing amiss.

Still holding on to Charlemagne, Caitlin walked to the back of the greenhouse. Everything there was secure, even to the loading gate door. She frowned and set the cat down, giving him a quick pat on the head. Charlemagne was usually so sedate, he bordered on being lazy. He was not a nervous or neurotic cat, she thought, although there was always a first time. Anyway, she couldn't quite shake a feeling of unease, especially when she headed toward the office and the cat followed right behind her, as if he were afraid to be alone.

That feeling was right on target, Caitlin realized when she unlocked and opened the door. The first thing she saw was the papers spread all over the desk and floor. Her heart began a quick thudding, and her breath caught when she saw the jagged-edged piece of glass that clung tenaciously to the bottom right corner of the window. The rest of the glass lay in long, glittering shards on the floor. A muddy footprint in the middle of the small table beneath the window was stark, mute testimony to what had happened.

Caitlin looked around for the metal petty cash box; she knew she had forgotten to lock it up last night. She wondered how much money had been in there—she hadn't counted it in the past two or three days. Probably fifty or a hundred. She saw the cash box lying upside down on the floor next to the safe and wasn't surprised to find it empty. She also noticed the calculator missing.

The next few hours passed in a blur. Caitlin filed a report with the police, explained the situation to Martha and K.C., and took care of her daily greenhouse chores. In the afternoon she filed another report with the detective assigned to the case and sorted through her files to see if any were gone. Through it all, she remained calm and professional.

It was nearly five-thirty before she put the last file back in the drawer. K.C. and Martha picked up their paychecks and left for the day. Caitlin ruffled through a stack of papers on her desk, more to have something to do than anything else. She found herself thinking of how composed and collected she felt. When Donna called a few minutes later, Caitlin was proud of how she described everything in very matter-of-fact terms.

"Are you okay?" Donna asked in concern.

"Oh, I'm just fine," Caitlin replied airily. "Nothing to worry about." Her gaze fell to her hand as it set a sheet of paper back on the desk. Her hand trembled, she realized with some surprise. She took a deep breath and flexed her fingers but couldn't seem to stop the tremors. She stared for endless moments, then the hot pressure of tears behind her eyes caused her to blink.

"Caitlin?" Donna sounded worried by Caitlin's silence. "Are you okay?" she asked again.

"No," Caitlin choked out as her whole body began to shake. "No, I'm not. I'm scared, Donna."

"I'll be right there," Donna told her immediately, and hung up the phone.

When she appeared ten minutes later, Caitlin was sitting in a chair in a corner, her feet drawn up beneath her. She cuddled Charlemagne, needing contact with another living creature.

Donna sat on the desk, facing the chair. "Hi" was all she said.

Caitlin looked up and tried to smile, but her lips quivered and her eyes filled with tears. "Oh, Donna, I'm so glad you came. I feel like I'm falling apart."

"Because of the break-in?"

Caitlin nodded. "I know it's silly. It's not the first time businesses in this end of town have been broken into, but I feel so—I feel—violated. I haven't felt like this since—well, you know."

"I know," Donna said gently. "Why don't you call Dr. Atlee?"

"She'd just think I was being foolish. I mean, it's just a break-in. They couldn't have gotten more than a hundred dollars or so. But somehow I keep remembering about—I keep remembering. I can't help it."

"I don't believe Dr. Atlee would think you foolish at all," Donna said, reaching over and laying a reassuring hand on Caitlin's arm. "This is bound to bring up unpleasant memories. I'm sure Dr.

Atlee would think it's completely normal, given the circumstances."

Caitlin sniffed. "Do you really think so?"

"I do. Here." Donna stood and handed Caitlin a tissue. "Why don't we go back to my house? We'll pick up Jordie at the sitter's and he can play with Patrick while you call Dr. Atlee. Okay?" She draped an arm around Caitlin's shoulders as they left.

Caitlin hung up the phone and reached over to take her glass of tea from the coffee table. She took a long swallow and set it back down before looking over at Donna.

"Well?"

Caitlin managed a little smile. "She said that my feelings were to be expected under the circumstances. That a robbery is an invasion of privacy, and that it's completely normal to think about what happened before."

"So do you feel better now?"

Caitlin sighed and brought her hands up to massage her temples. "I don't know. A little, maybe."

"Why don't you stay here for the night? Jordie and Patrick would both love it, you know, and I don't think you ought to be home alone tonight."

Caitlin was silent for a moment. "Thanks, Donna. Maybe I will," she said slowly. "I don't want to be alone right now either. I guess I ought to go home and pick up some clothes for both Jordan and me though. Are you sure it won't be any trouble?" she asked, although she knew Donna would have made room for her and Jordan even if it meant pitching a tent in the backyard.

"No trouble at all." Donna smiled. "You can be the guinea pig that checks out the new mattress in the guest room. Rick picked one up at some warehouse sale. Heaven knows, it could be as lumpy as Grandma's gravy."

"Jordie?" Caitlin called up the stairs.

Jordan came bounding down. "Can't I stay longer, Mom? While you're out with Max and all?"

"Oh, good heavens!" Caitlin exclaimed in consternation. "I forgot." She dug through her purse and found her address book, then looked up Max's number and dialed, ignoring Donna's sudden look of interest.

"No answer," she muttered, hanging up the telephone. He'd probably gotten disgusted with waiting for her and taken someone else out. Surely he had dozens of women ready to jump at a date with him. Caitlin ignored the pang that thought caused.

Only after Donna walked Caitlin out to her van did she remark, "So you had a date with Max tonight, hmm?"

Caitlin sighed and shifted uncomfortably in the seat. "Not really a date. Just dinner."

"A dinner alone with a man is a date in my book."

"All right. Yes, I had a date," Caitlin admitted.

"Gee, I thought you didn't date."

"I don't. At least not anymore," Caitlin said flatly as she started her vehicle. When Donna gave a cheery wave, Caitlin stuck her head out the window and added, "I'll be back in a little while."

When Caitlin pulled up into her driveway, she stifled a twinge of disappointment that Max wasn't waiting for her. Not that she had expected him to, she assured herself, and not that she wanted him to. It would be far better for Max to get involved with someone who was ready for whatever kind of relationship he had in mind.

And tonight Caitlin had had to admit to herself that it would be a long time, if ever, before she forgot the helplessness, the fear. She suddenly realized how much she had nurtured the hope that somehow Max might be a part of her future. But there would be no future unless she dealt with a past that she couldn't bear to face. She refused to burden Max with her problems, so until she could deal with them herself, she wouldn't see Max.

She didn't know how she would ever get used to not seeing him though. She'd known him only a few weeks, but he had insinuated himself into her life so thoroughly that there was nowhere she could go, little she could do that wouldn't make her think of him. Her heart contracted painfully at the thought of the empty days ahead.

With her mind so full of thoughts, she almost didn't see him when she opened the front door. She'd walked halfway across the living room before doing an about-face and looking over at the sofa.

Max sat there in the dark, his face illuminated by the streetlight that shone through the window, his feet propped up on the coffee table. "Finally decided to come home?" he asked casually.

"What are you doing in my house? How did you get in?"

Max shrugged. "Where there's a will, there's a way. So, where were you?"

"I didn't see your car outside."

Max said evenly, "I waited here an hour for you. When you didn't show up, I went by the greenhouse. My car had an argument with the big pothole next to the loading platform. I had it towed and took a cab back. Where were you?"

"I did call you and didn't get an answer," Caitlin said defensively.

"That's nice. Where were you?" he repeated.

Caitlin took a deep breath and walked over to stand next to the window. "I was at Donna's."

"Donna's." Max nodded. "I see. Why?"

Caitlin fidgeted with the edge of the ruffled curtain. "I'm really sorry you were inconvenienced."

"Why were you at Donna's?" Max's voice was still calm, but it held an underlying current that told Caitlin he was losing patience.

"Jordan is still at Donna's. I came only to pick up a change of clothes for tomorrow. He's spending the night there. I am too." Nervously, she dropped the curtain and turned toward the stairs.

She hadn't taken two steps when Max shot up off the sofa and stood directly in front of her. "Why were you at Donna's, Caitlin? Were you trying to avoid me?" His voice started out sharp, then gentled. "It was only a dinner date, Cait. I wouldn't have pushed you for anything else."

To Caitlin's horror, her eyes filled with tears and she quickly averted her head, but not before Max saw.

"What happened, Caitie?"

Her knees weak from the sudden welling of emotion, Caitlin sank wearily down onto the sofa. "Someone broke into the greenhouse."

"Good Lord!" Max sat down beside her and reached over, taking her hand between both of his. "Were you there when it happened? Did they take anything?"

She shook her head, blinking more tears away. "No, I wasn't there. It happened last night, and I think they got about a hundred dollars or so. They took my calculator. It was an old calculator, so it couldn't have been worth much. It's just that . . ." Aware she was rambling, Caitlin stopped and stared down at the floor for a long while, then finally added in a strangled whisper, "All I could think of was how I felt violated all over again."

Max closed his eyes against the pain that stabbed him at those words, then pulled her into his arms. "Nothing, and no one, will ever hurt you again, Caitie", he said. He repeated the statement over and over. It was his litany, his prayer, his promise.

Caitlin forgot her resolve to stay out of Max's life. Being in his arms felt so safe, so warm, so secure, and she reveled in those feelings. She savored every second he held her, storing memories for the long, lonely days ahead. She relished the clean, fresh scent of him, the beating of his heart beneath her cheek, the warmth of his body, the firm but yielding ridges of muscle, the way his arms cradled but didn't confine. His embrace was a warm, living haven.

It took her a nearly superhuman effort to gently disengage herself. She'd never be able to say what she had to say if he kept touching her. "I'm glad you're here, Max," she began, looking down at her hands, which she had folded together in her lap. "We need to talk."

"So let's talk." Max brushed a strand of hair from her cheek.

She ducked her head away and cleared her throat. The words wouldn't come, so she took a deep breath and shifted away from him, somehow forcing out the words. "I can't see you anymore."

Whatever Max had been expecting Caitlin to say, it wasn't that. "What?"

"I said, I can't see you anymore," Caitlin repeated, stronger this time.

"What in God's name are you talking about?" Max suddenly felt as if he were adrift in the middle of an ocean with no compass or idea of where he was headed.

"Max, I honestly thought I was ready for—for, well, ready to—" She floundered to a stop, not sure how to proceed.

Max reached over and took hold of one of her hands. "Talk to me, Caitie. Tell me," he said firmly. "I think you owe me that much."

She did owe him that, she thought. Owed him the truth about what had happened so many years before and how it had scarred her. She shut her eyes briefly against the pain, then opened her mouth, intending to tell him, but couldn't make the words come out. She took a deep breath, swallowed, and tried again—and failed once more.

She began to get angry. She shouldn't have to say anything if she didn't want to. Max had no right to insist, especially since he'd be out of her life in another week or two. He'd soon tire of dealing with her and move on to easier game. She stiffened her back. "My reasons aren't important. But the fact remains that I think it would be best for us not to see each other anymore."

"Don't you think you owe me an explanation?" Max was confused. Now he didn't even know which ocean he was in.

"I don't owe you anything. My reasons have nothing to do with you," Caitlin replied stiffly.

"Anything to do with you has everything to do with me." Max's voice was low but intense.

Why couldn't he just leave it alone? Why did he keep pushing? Caitlin gritted her teeth. "Let it be, Max. Just let it be."

"Caitlin, I only want to—"

"I know what you want to do. You want to meddle in my life." The desperate urge to make him leave before he got too close to the truth made her words sharper than she intended.

Max was stunned. The ocean had turned into a raging hurricane. "I'm only concerned, Caitlin," he said carefully. "I know we can't have a relationship until—"

"That's right! We can't have a relationship!" Caitlin broke in and jumped to her feet. Please leave, she begged silently. Her control was so fragile, so tenuous, she was afraid it would shatter at any moment. And she was afraid that once that happened, she'd never be able to put the pieces back together. She turned her back to him. "Max, please just go."

Max stood, his fists clenched at his sides, but with an effort he managed to keep his voice gentle. "I want only to help, Caitlin."

"I don't want your help! I don't need it! I just want you to go now!"

Max laid a hand on her shoulder, but she stepped away. He sighed in frustration and stuffed his hands into his pockets. "I can see I need to give you a little time," he said. "I'll call you tomorrow, then."

"Please don't. There's no reason."

"There's every reason."

Caitlin's dark ghost reared its head then, and she felt a trembling begin deep inside. She had to get Max out of there before she exposed all her emotional bruises. Holding her fear at bay with every ounce of strength she had, she faced him. "What's the matter, Max? Why can't you believe that I simply don't want to see you anymore? I'm sure you're not used to being turned down by women, but maybe I'm one who just doesn't happen to find you irresistible. It's possible, you know." Her voice wasn't shaking, thank God.

"Maybe," he said, "but I don't believe you. I don't believe you for a minute."

"Well, you'll just have to, won't you?" Caitlin could feel her already flimsy control beginning to fray, so she walked to the door and opened it. "Good night, Max."

He walked to her, fixing her with a sharp, burning gaze. "This isn't over, Caitlin. Not by a long shot."

"It *is* over, Max. Good night."

Without another word Max strode through the door and slammed it shut behind him, the sound reverberating in the air. The tremors overcame her and she sank down on the sofa, her legs no longer able to support her. Wrapping her arms around herself, she sat for a long time. Finally, she buried her face in her hands and wept.

Eight

"What do you mean, you're out of angelica? . . . Do you know anybody else who has it? Martin's is a good customer of mine and I don't want to let them down. I already cut their order of Siberian ginseng. . . . Well, I guess I'll just have to check over at Organifarms. . . . Thanks."

Caitlin sighed with frustration and hung up the phone. She tossed the pencil she'd been chewing on down on the desk and massaged her temples. Today was just another day in what had already been a long, miserable week.

K.C. had caught his mother's flu and was out sick, so Caitlin was behind in filling orders. One grower had backed out of a commitment for Siberian ginseng. Jordie had gotten a D on a spelling test he had forgotten to study for. She'd gotten a ticket for an expired inspection sticker on her van.

And it had been a week since she had seen or heard from Max. The longest, lousiest, most wretched week of her life. It didn't help that she kept getting accusing looks from Jordan every time she gave him a vague answer about where Max was.

Every time she thought of Max, missed Max, ached for Max, she knew she had only herself to blame. That was the worst of all. She had been too chicken to fight for what she wanted. And she was just now realizing how much she wanted Max in her life.

She hadn't believed that she'd ever be able to feel for a man what she felt for Max. He was the kindest, gentlest, sexiest, most annoying, irritating man she'd ever met, and he made her feel wonderfully alive. What had her cowardice cost her?

Coward. That word began to loom larger and larger. Every time she looked in the mirror, she imagined big fluorescent yellow letters spelling it out on her forehead. "Caitlin is a coward, a weakling, a chicken."

Even Donna was no help. She called Caitlin a coward right to her face. Dr. Atlee hemmed and hawed in her aggravatingly professional way and said that if Caitlin felt like a coward, then it was up to Caitlin to change that.

But how? Caitlin stared out the brand-new window in her office and absently watched a pair of finches flutter around the bird feeder she'd hung outside. Had she been a coward all her life? Or had it begun seven years before when she'd been made to feel impotent and weak? When was it that she'd been left fearing conflict of any sort? Why did she still carry those feelings of powerlessness all these years later?

She stood up. Seven years was long enough to carry around that kind of burden, she decided. It was time to talk to Max, to find out if he was indeed the kind of man she thought, hoped, he was. If he couldn't deal with what she had to tell him, she might as well find out now rather than spend the rest of her life wondering what would have happened "if."

"Martha." She poked her head out the office door and called to the prematurely gray woman who was cataloguing a new shipment of rootstock.

"Yes?"

"Will you be okay if I leave you to close up today? I need to leave early."

"Of course."

"Just be careful and don't overdo. I don't want you having a relapse."

"I'll be fine." Martha smiled and waved a hand toward the door. "Don't you worry about a thing, honey. You just scoot along."

Don't worry about a thing? Caitlin thought to herself. She felt as if she had the worries of the world on her shoulders and it was all due to that man! Sighing, she slung the strap of her purse over her shoulder and went home.

As soon as she walked in, she called Donna. "I'm going to talk to Max," she said.

"It's about time!"

"Can you pick Jordie up at the sitter's?"

"You bet. As a matter of fact, just in case you're late getting home, why don't we just plan on him spending the night? Patrick would love it."

"Thanks, Donna," Caitlin said with a sigh. "I hope I'm doing the right thing."

"Truth is always right. It'll all work out."

"I hope so. Thanks, Donna." Caitlin gently set the receiver down.

She spent nearly thirty minutes contemplating her wardrobe. She changed clothes twice before selecting a short nut-brown skirt and crocheted cream sweater. The colors complemented her brown eyes and ivory skin, and the style made her feel flirty and feminine. Heaven knows, she was going to need all the help she could get, she thought as she dialed Max's office.

"Shore Efficiency Consultants, your time is our business. May I help you?"

Here goes nothing. Caitlin cleared her throat. "I, well, I'd like to see Mr. Shore this afternoon."

"I'm sorry, Mr. Shore is booked for the rest of the day. I'll be glad to schedule you as soon as possible. Let's see, how about tomorrow morning at eleven-thirty?"

Caitlin's heart sank. "That'll be fine, I guess."

"Your name, please?"

"Love. Caitlin Love."

"Ms. Love?" The secretary's voice relayed renewed interest. "Ah, I believe I just had a cancellation and can work you in, oh, let's say about thirty minutes?"

Caitlin's heart leapt from her stomach up into her throat. "I'll be there."

When she arrived in his building, she stood outside the glass door to his suite of offices for a long time, trying to get her erratic breathing under control. She frowned at her reflection in the glass, then straightened an imaginary crease in her sleeve and wiped her sweaty palms on her skirt. Sticking out her jaw in determination, she pushed open the door.

The first thing she saw was a tall, slender brunette with Max's eyes. Caitlin simply stared until the woman said, "Ms. Love?"

"Um, yes." She had to be Max's sister.

The woman stood and held out a hand. "Hi, I'm

Patsy Shore Elliott. I've heard a lot about you," she said with frank curiosity.

The two women shook hands, then Patsy waved at the chair next to her desk. "Please, sit down. My brother is currently tied up on the phone. Conference call." She propped her elbows on the desk and leaned forward. "So, I guess you're the reason Max has been biting at the furniture all week."

Caitlin could feel color slowly creep from beneath her collar and up her cheeks. "I beg your pardon?"

"Not that there's anything wrong with that, mind you. A little furniture-chewing is good for you. Sharpens the teeth and all that."

Caitlin squirmed uncomfortably, not sure what to say. "What makes you think I'm the reason?" she finally managed to ask.

"Well, when my brother the grouch slouched into the office Monday morning, the first thing he said was that if a certain Ms. Love called, I was to tell her he was out of town. And the second thing he said was to change that. If a certain Ms. Love called, *he* wanted the pleasure of telling her he was out of town."

Caitlin winced. "I'm sorry. I—I don't know what to say."

Patsy smiled, her eyes twinkling. "You don't have to say anything to me, but I sure hope you're gonna say something to Max that will change his prickly attitude before he leaves teeth marks in the chair legs."

In spite of her nervousness and embarrassment, Caitlin smiled a little at Patsy's brash, amiable humor. She decided that she liked Max's sister very much. Just then the intercom on Patsy's desk buzzed, a sound that made Caitlin jump.

"Patsy," Max's voice crackled over the electronic device, "when Mr. McKenna gets here, send him straight in, please."

Patsy gave a conspiratorial wink to Caitlin and pressed the button to answer, "Your next appointment is already here."

"Send him in."

Caitlin's knees were shaky as she stood and crossed the few feet to Max's private office. Her sweaty hand slipped on the polished brass doorknob and she had to tighten her grip to twist it open. She glanced back at Patsy, who gave her an encouraging thumbs-up signal.

"Mr. McKenna." Max, who'd been sitting with his back to the door, stood and held out his hand. When he saw who it was, his features hardened and his hand dropped slowly to his side. He was silent for a moment, as if searching for the right words, before saying formally, "Caitlin. I'm afraid you've dropped by at an inconvenient time. I have another appointment due any minute."

Caitlin would have turned tail and run had she not seen a flicker of something, pain maybe, in Max's eyes before the impenetrable mask dropped down. "Your secretary worked me in."

Max immediately punched the button on his intercom. "Patsy, when Mr. McKenna comes in, please have him wait in the office next door."

"Gee, Max, I'm afraid Mr. McKenna won't be in at all this afternoon."

"What?"

"As a matter of fact, I've rescheduled all of your afternoon appointments. And since you have such a light afternoon schedule, I'm leaving early. *Ciao!*"

"Patsy. Patsy." When she didn't respond, he

strode out of his office only to see the flip of her skirt hem as she went out the door. He turned suspicious eyes back to Caitlin. "Just what did you and my sister cook up?"

Caitlin, her cheeks burning, held up her hands. "All I did was call for an appointment. Anything your sister did, she did on her own."

"Well, you have your appointment," Max said flatly. "What do you want?" His eyes lit on the length of leg revealed by the alluringly short shirt, and he swallowed hard, hastily averting his gaze. He had wondered how she would look in a skirt. Now he knew. Legs like that could turn even the most jaded playboy's head.

Caitlin's fingernails dug into the material of her clutch purse, but her voice was steady. "I need to talk to you, Max."

He cleared his throat, his eyes still focused somewhere past her. "If it's about the greenhouse, I've decided it might be best to assign Emily Jane to—"

"It isn't about business. It's about you and me." Caitlin licked her sandpaper-dry lips, trying in vain to moisten them.

Max's gaze quickly swung to her face. "You and me?"

Caitlin nodded. "I—I owe you an apology. I wasn't fair to you."

Her voice was so low that Max could hardly make out her words, but he heard enough to want to leap to her and pull her into his arms. He controlled himself though, and instead leaned back against the doorjamb and stuffed his itchy hands into his pockets. "And?"

Drat! He wasn't going to make this easy, was he? Not that she deserved it easy, she thought ruefully, but he could have been nicer about it. "And I—we need to talk."

"So talk."

"Not here."

"Well, it just so happens I have a free afternoon." The barest hint of Max's familiar wry smile flitted across his face. "Your place or mine?"

They chose Max's place because Max suggested it and Caitlin was too caught up in her own thoughts to suggest otherwise. Max decided Caitlin should go with him in his car, and again, she didn't argue. She didn't speak a single word the entire ride, but Max couldn't help but notice that every muscle in her body was tense and ready—to fight or to flee. He didn't know which.

His heart ached at the sight of her pale face and trembling hands, but he couldn't let her off the hook, not this time. Their entire future together depended on what and how much she said.

Oh, God, I don't know if I can do it! Caitlin thought in anguish as they walked into his house. How could she bear to say the ugly words? How could she bear the look on Max's face when he heard them?

They sat on the sofa, side by side, Caitlin wondering desperately if she could somehow avoid the truth. Finally, Max reached over a hand and laid it on top of hers. "Tell me, Caitie," he urged gently.

"I'm afraid," she whispered. "Max, I'm so afraid. I don't know if I can make the words come out. I haven't said them in a long time."

"I know it's hard, sweet Cait. But you have to try. I need to know."

Caitlin knew he was right. She stiffened her

back and took a deep breath. "Seven years ago, when I was seventeen and a senior in high school, I was pretty shy so I, um, didn't date much. You can imagine how surprised I felt when the most popular boy in town, a sophomore in college, asked me out during Christmas break."

Max stared at the far wall, seeing in his mind a younger, more idealistic Caitlin with the promise of her woman's beauty already beginning to show. A shy, innocent seventeen-year-old. He closed his eyes in a brief moment of panic. Did he really want to hear about the destruction of that innocence?

"My friends couldn't believe it. Neither could I. Part of me was so flattered that he'd asked me out. The other part was scared. He was everything I wasn't—wealthy, self-assured, a member of the 'in' crowd. I just couldn't imagine what he wanted with a bookworm like me." Caitlin stood abruptly and walked over to stand by the big picture window.

She stared out the window for a long while, then continued, her voice flat. "He took me to a very elegant restaurant. I certainly wasn't dressed properly in my little Sunday-school dress—most of the women there were wearing cocktail dresses. Br-Brad,"—Caitlin had to force the name out—"Brad said I looked fine. After dinner we went dancing at a really fancy nightclub. We were both well under twenty-one, but the manager took one look at Brad and I guess he could read the money. He never said a word. I was so impressed."

She fell silent again, but Max could see her knuckles whiten as her fists clenched at her sides. A tear ran down her cheek, then another, but when she spoke, her voice was quiet and steady. "When we left the club, Brad drove me to a little spot overlooking the lake. He said it was time to pay up."

"Caitlin," Max broke in, "you don't have to go on with this."

"Oh, but I do. For my sake as well as yours," she said. "I told him that I didn't think it was funny and demanded he take me home. I told him to stop, I begged him to stop, but—"

"No more." Max jumped to his feet and covered the distance separating them in two steps. He put his hands on her shoulders and turned her to face him. "You don't have to say any more, Caitie. I know now."

"No!" She nearly screamed the word as she pushed his hands away. "I have to say it. He raped me, Max. He raped me." The words seemed to echo around the room. She gave a short, ugly laugh. "He took me home afterward as if nothing had happened. He even said he'd call me over spring break. Maybe we could do it again."

"Oh, God," Max exclaimed. "Oh, God." His whole body burned with incredible anger and pain. "You weren't to blame, Cait."

Caitlin slapped the wall with the palm of her hand. "I know that now, but he was so matter-of-fact about it that I spent days wondering what I had done to lead him on. What I had done to ask for it."

Max ran a hand over her hair. When she didn't shy away, he did it again. "What did you do?"

"I finally decided that it wasn't my fault, that no girl should have to do what she doesn't want to do, and I went to the police. But by then it was all over school that Caitlin Love was an easy mark. All I had was a torn dress and my word against his money. I got a ruined reputation. He got sent to

Europe." Caitlin lifted her gaze then and met Max's eyes. "My own father couldn't handle it. He kicked me out when he found out I was pregnant."

"Jordan." Max felt as though he'd been punched in the stomach. That bright, curious, delightful little boy was the result of such violence? He couldn't say anything more, but he pulled Caitlin into his arms and held her tightly, burying his face in her neck.

Her arms slid around his shoulders and held on as if for dear life.

The burning tears that she had kept at bay with an iron will now poured out in bitter healing release. Max cradled her in his embrace, his body absorbing the force of her anger, anguish, and fear, while his mind tried to absorb the reality of what his beautiful Caitlin had endured. He wondered briefly why Caitlin hadn't had an abortion, then realized she was too much of a nurturer to have even considered the option.

When the sobs finally eased to snuffles, Max led Caitlin back to the sofa and sat down, pulling her into his lap. She stiffened for an instant, then relaxed, allowing him to hold her and wipe the tears from her cheeks. He tilted her face up, pressed a light kiss on her forehead, then asked, "And now, sweet Cait?"

She took a deep breath. "And now? I don't know. I love Jordan more than anything, but I've been unable to deal with . . . other feelings. I was in therapy for four years and still couldn't handle a normal date. It's only been during the past couple of years that I've been able to go out, as long as the man didn't get too close."

She smiled tremulously. "Then along came Maximillian Tobias Shore. He didn't take no for an answer and he made me feel again." She paused, wiping the back of her hand across one cheek. "Granted, he often made me feel angry," she said, smiling again, "but at least I wasn't numb anymore."

"Why did you try to push me away?"

She dropped her gaze. "What happened last week only proved to me that I may never be able to get past the bad memories and build a future. You need someone who can."

"But I want you, Cait."

"Max." She struggled halfheartedly to get up out of his lap, but he stopped her with his hands on her shoulders. She shook her head ruefully. "If you were really smart, you'd run like crazy."

"If you were really smart, you wouldn't presume to tell me what I need or want." Max kissed her nose. "I'm a big boy now and I've been picking out my own clothes for years. I think I can pick out my own lady too. I want you, and if I have to fight every single solitary private dragon of yours to get you, I will. I'm not going anywhere, Caitie. You can't chase me away, you can't send me away, and you can't shut me out."

"I was afraid I had chased you away," she murmured.

"Why did you think that?"

"Because of this past week. You hadn't called or anything."

Max hugged Caitlin and rested his head atop hers. "I was angry. And I was hurt. But I was already trying to decide whether to march over to that greenhouse and take you by storm or whether to send flowers and candy and try to woo you back."

She pulled back enough to see his face clearly. A smile played around her lips. "I don't eat candy."

"Carob-coated almonds."

"Oh. Well, I suppose you could try the flowers and candy if you wanted to."

"Why? I've got you now."

Caitlin's face became serious. "Max, I don't know if this is going to change anything between us. I don't know if I'm ready for a relationship. But even more than that, I don't know if I ever will be. I'm not the right woman for you."

"Let me decide that for myself, sweet Cait."

A sudden thought occurred to her, and Caitlin again tried to stand, this time succeeding. She stepped back a pace or two, needing some room. "Max, if you have any ideas about me being some sort of reclamation project, then you can just forget—"

"Caitlin!" Max shot to his feet, anger and hurt warring in his expression. He stood breathing hard for a moment, like a bull deciding whether or not to charge. Finally, he gave a deep sigh and shoved his hands into his pockets. His voice was surprisingly mild when he said, "If you think I'm seeing you as my Boy Scout project of the week, then perhaps I need to enlighten you as to my real feelings." He took a step closer to her, then another, his blue eyes gleaming.

Sapphire? Indigo? Turquoise? Caitlin was mesmerized by his eyes as he moved even closer.

"Now, let's see," Max mused as he threaded the fingers of one hand through her tousled curls. "I need to find a way to convince you that my interest in you is purely personal and has nothing to do with pity or sympathy." He brought up the other hand to cradle the side of her face. "I wonder what I could do to convince you?" he said as his gaze dropped to her lips.

"Max." She had to tell him that she didn't want this right now. It was too soon after reliving the old memories. She had to tell him. She would. Later.

He bent his head and his lips slid over hers with the smoothness of satin against satin. He entreated, he teased, he compelled, and she could no more keep herself from responding than she could keep herself from breathing. It felt right. It felt good. It felt perfect.

His tongue played over her lips, asking but not demanding entrance. And she supplied it, her lips parted beneath his gentle persuasion. Her hands wound through his thick hair, pulling him closer.

Max reveled in her response to him. His kiss grew more insistent as his fingers moved over her back, then moved around front.

The weight of her breasts filled his hands, and he savored the feel of the soft, pliant mounds. He wanted more, so much more, but she gave an inarticulate moan that reminded him that Caitlin had already taken one giant step. He would not ask her to take another just yet.

With iron will he brought his raging desire under control. His hands slid to her waist and he pulled back just far enough so that she could see the desire still flaring in his eyes. "Just so you'll know," he said, his voice husky with suppressed passion, "I want you more than I've ever wanted anything. Don't ever doubt that. But the next move is yours, my sweet Cait."

Nine

Caitlin couldn't stop staring at his eyes, his beautiful eyes. She could feel his gaze as strongly as if he were actually touching her. Her head told her to pull away, but her body longed to go back into his embrace.

Her breasts felt heavy and swollen, and she knew that only the touch of his hands would ease the ache. Her mouth felt bereft, and only the touch of his lips would assuage the hunger. "Max," she said. Just one word, but it contained a wealth of longing.

The husky timbre of her voice slid over his heated flesh like velvet and it brought every nerve ending to throbbing life. Max had to clench his hands into fists to keep from reaching for her. The choice had to be hers. He could feel her indecision and forced himself to stand still even though he was sure his whole body radiated the force of his desperate need.

Please come to me, sweet Cait, he thought over and over as if his thoughts could somehow make it happen. His heart pounded when she swayed closer to him, then took that one step that brought them together.

"Max?"

In her face he saw a curious and moving mixture of longing and fear. Instead of pulling her into his arms the way he wanted to, he took both her hands and cradled them in his.

"Caitie," he said tenderly.

"I'm afraid," she admitted, so quietly that Max had to strain to hear it.

Silence fell, a hazy, sensual silence. "Of making love with me?" he finally asked.

Caitlin nodded. "Yes. And of not making love with you."

His eyes bored into hers and his breath quickened. "Which are you the most afraid of, sweet Cait?"

Her cheeks flushed enchantingly, but her gaze never left his. "Of not making love with you." She leaned her head forward, resting it on his chest. "Please help me, Max."

Awed by the gift she was offering him, he brought his hands up to cradle her face. "Caitlin, I will never do anything to hurt you. I promise."

His mind searched desperately for anything he could say to reassure her. And then, with an intuition born of love and need, he knew. This time had to be as different from her first time as it could be. "All you ever have to say is stop and I'll stop, Caitlin. I promise. Believe me."

She nodded and waited for him to kiss her. But he didn't. He stood there looking at her with a mixed expression on his face—quizzical, tender, intense, and patient. Caitlin's heart turned over.

He was waiting for her to make the first move. But she didn't know if she could.

Caitlin tried to coax herself and still couldn't make herself reach out to him. Finally, Max gently took her right hand. He lifted it to his lips, pressed a kiss on the back of it, then brought it to the knot in his tie.

A tremulous smile lit her face as she slowly loosened the tie. When she pulled it off, she was rewarded by Max's sharply indrawn breath. But he remained still.

Her forehead creased in thought. So that's the way it was going to be, was it? Her fingers toyed with the top button of his shirt, then opened it. Max's back stiffened. She undid the second and third buttons. Max's hands clenched at his sides. After the fourth button her fingers slipped inside and caught in silky golden brown curls. Beads of sweat broke out on Max's forehead, and his hands moved to cover hers.

"Do you know what you're doing?" he asked hoarsely.

"I'm seducing you, I think. Am I doing it right?"

"You seduce me just by breathing, but yeah, you could teach a class in it."

"Really?"

"Really." His voice was little more than a groan. "Ah, Caitie, kiss me. More than anything, I need you to kiss me."

Slowly, her hands urged his head down. Their lips met, hers hesitant and seeking, his sure and gently. Hers parted beneath his, but he didn't move in, he simply waited, his mouth warm and hungry, but passive.

Caitlin felt a sharp stab of impatience and she thought of how long it had been since she had wanted anything this much. If she ever had. And now she was going to have to take control to get it.

Heady excitement shot through her. She felt exhilarated. She felt powerful. Powerful? She paused, suddenly understanding what Max was doing. He was *letting* her take control. A wave of tenderness swept over her, giving her the strength she hadn't been able to find before.

She stood on tiptoe to fit her body more intimately to his. The tip of her tongue teased the corners of his mouth before making little forays inside, inviting him to follow suit.

Max's breath caught in his throat and his hands swept slowly down her back, then up again to thread through her silky curls, curls that always seemed bedroom-tousled.

He slanted his mouth over hers with an urgency held firmly in check. He intended to keep it in check even if it killed him. And the way his need for her burned through his veins like acid, he felt as if it just might.

Caitlin felt his hands toying with the bottom of her sweater, his fingers darting beneath it to run lightly over her waist. But the teasing wasn't enough. It did nothing to fill the longing that raged within her. Pulling away slightly, she took his hands, then slowly urged them upward, drawing the sweater with them.

He continued to draw the sweater up and over her head, tossing it aside. The lace of her bra was a sensual barrier to his exploring fingers as they found and caressed her creamy mounds. Her gasp of pleasure told him without words that she wanted more, and he reached gentle fingers behind her to unhook the clasp of her bra.

Her gasp, this time, was one of surprise, and

Max felt her hands clutch his shoulders. He paused in his explorations to lavish caresses on her face. He ran his fingers down her cheeks and across her lips, following with his lips.

Only when her grip eased and she began to urge him closer did he let his hands touch her soft breasts. Rosy nipples hardened immediately, inviting him to taste. "So beautiful," Max murmured against her skin, "you're so beautiful." He took one swollen nipple, then the other, into his mouth and bathed each with his tongue.

"Max," Caitlin whimpered, feeling her knees begin to buckle with delicious weakness.

"Do you want more?" Max's voice enveloped her, a whisper that promised untold pleasures.

"Yes, oh, yes."

Max held out his hand, a smile of tender yearning on his face. "Then take my hand, sweet Cait, and lead me to bed."

Caitlin took him up the stairs, then paused in the hall. "Which room is yours?" When Max indicated his answer, Caitlin led him inside, stopping next to the bed. Her heart pounded with anticipation as she stroked his chest, the golden-brown curls tickling her fingers. She slid his shirt from his shoulders, gratified at the low moan that issued from his throat.

His muscles tense beneath her touch, Max stood still, letting her dictate what would happen next. Caitlin's hands, more sure than they had been a few minutes before, moved to the buckle of his belt. As she undid it, she felt a tremor run through his body matching the one that ran through hers. "Touch me, Max," she breathed.

His eyes held hers in a gaze so intense she could feel its heat as he unbuttoned her skirt. He slid the garment, her half slip, and pantyhose down in one sweeping movement, leaving her clad only in panties. At the cool air that wafted over her, she stirred apprehensively and looked down, but Max reached out one hand to tilt her chin back up. "Look at me, Cait. Don't stop looking at me."

She whispered, "I feel . . . I feel so vulnerable."

"I know, sweet Cait. I know." He quickly removed his trousers and briefs and stood before her, his eyes still holding hers. "See? I'm as vulnerable as you now. More, because you can hide how you feel. I can't." He reached out and took her hands, bringing them to his chest.

"Touch me, Caitie," he pleaded softly. "Touch me and see what your touch does to me."

She spread her hands over his chest, haltingly tentatively. When his muscles jerked beneath her fingers and Caitlin felt the rapid pounding of his heart, her caresses became more certain.

"Dear God!" Max groaned, and Caitlin felt him shudder. "Let me love you, sweet Cait. I need you more than I need my next breath."

At those words Caitlin very gently pushed him until he sat down on the edge of the bed. She moved next to him and threaded her fingers through his silky brown hair. She urged his head down to hers, parting her lips immediately beneath his. Her caresses became even more insistent, more daring.

It wasn't until she lightly feathered her fingers across his arousal that Max took the initiative. His tongue plunging deep into her mouth, he urged her back until she lay on the bed. Then his hands staked their own claim on her body. Every time Caitlin's eyes fluttered closed, Max made her open them and look at him.

When his mouth paid sweet homage to her breasts, he watched her brown eyes grow soft and hazy. When his seeking fingers removed her panties and discovered the womanly secrets between her thighs, he saw her eyes widen with pleasure at his touch. And when he used his lips and hands to bring her to the brink of fulfillment, he watched her eyes darken to almost black.

He left her side to reach for something on the nightstand, and Caitlin murmured with disappointment at the unwanted distance between them. He pulled her back into his arms and she shifted against him, trying to get closer still.

But when he began to press inside her, Caitlin shut her eyes tightly and stiffened. "Caitlin," Max said hoarsely, "open your eyes and look at me, sweetheart. It's only me and I'll never hurt you. You know that. I'll never hurt you. I want only to love you, Caitie. Let me in, sweetheart. Let me in."

Gradually the tenseness left her and she began to relax. Only then did Max enter her fully. His breathing harsh and heavy, he lay still for a moment, to regain what little of his control remained and to give her a chance to get accustomed to him. He felt as if a sacred charge had been given to him: to erase all the bad memories and replace them with ones of gentleness and love and passion. When she shifted her body beneath him, he moved against her, whispering sweet words and reassurances all the while.

He kissed her, a slow, deep kiss that stole her breath away and gave it back again. His hands touched and fondled whatever they could reach, as if they couldn't get enough of her. The warmth that was stealing through her body grew hotter with each of his strokes until she thought she'd burst into flames.

"Max?" She clutched his shoulders with her hands.

"Yes, sweetheart. Let go. I'll catch you."

When she finally found release moments later, tears ran down her cheeks at the sheer beauty of it, and she spoke Max's name over and over.

Max then released the steel grip on his control and tumbled headlong into pleasure. He arched his back and cried out her name before collapsing on her, his face buried in her neck.

Overwhelmed by the intensity of his feelings, he lay still, catching his breath, and reveling in the way their bodies felt pressed together. He realized that the only time he felt right, complete, was when they were together, as if each were one half of a whole.

Without releasing her he rolled to one side and levered himself up on one elbow. He needed to look at her face but was afraid of what he'd see. When he saw the silvery tears on her cheeks, his stomach knotted. But the look in her eyes was soft and warm and hazy with satisfaction.

"Thank you for making it beautiful," she said softly.

Max pressed a sweet kiss on her lips. "We made it beautiful, sweetheart, not me. And just so you'll know, I've never felt like this before."

"Neither have I." When a smile spread over his face, she said, "A conquering-hero smile if I ever saw one."

"Really?" He nuzzled the side of her neck, tasting the saltiness of her skin.

"Mm-hmm," she turned her head slightly, affording him better access. "Definitely."

"I've always fancied myself a hero type." His smile became less victorious and more possessive as his hand settled over the softness of her breast.

Caitlin said breathlessly, "Fighting dragons and all that?"

His smile faded, replaced by a look of intensity. "I'll fight all the dragons I have to, Caitie, because I've just discovered that the princess in the castle tower is worth all the battles." He bent his head to run his tongue around one rosy nipple.

"Ah, is, ah, that a dragon you're after?"

She could feel another smile curve his lips. "I think so. Shh, now, let me see if I can catch the rascal." He made a few more swirls with his tongue before lightly nipping at her with his teeth. "There, I think I've caught him." He grinned.

"I don't know. I think he's getting away." Her eyes shone with amusement.

Max was enchanted by this playful side of Caitlin. He hoped to see more of it. A lot more. "I'll just have to stop him, won't I?" With that, he captured one tight bud between his lips, sucking gently.

Her breath escaped in an audible sigh. "Yes, I definitely think you've got him this time."

"Not yet. I won't be satisfied till I've taken the castle by storm." His fingers slid underneath her to cup her smooth bottom, while his lips continued to nibble at her breast.

"Max?" she breathed.

"Yes, sweetheart."

"Be careful that the dragon doesn't spring a surprise attack on you."

"Surprise attack?"

"Yes. Like this." With unexpected strength and agility she pushed him onto his back. "You see, sometimes the dragon fights back." She flicked her tongue across his tight nipple. His body jerked in response and his eyes opened wide at the look on Caitlin's face. It was so supremely, so powerfully female that it took his breath away.

Caitlin felt alive, more alive than she'd felt in seven years. She felt young and strong and feminine, and gloried in those feelings. She didn't know if she could find the words to tell Max how she felt, but she could do everything in her power to show him. She lowered her head to his, her eyes gleaming.

While her lips busily seduced his, her hands discovered Max's hard, lean body. It was a perfect complement to her softer one, and she found pleasure in running her hands over the taut cords of muscle in his shoulders and chest. Her fingers tangled in the silky gold-brown curls that dusted his chest, then swept across each flat brown nipple.

When Max groaned she felt the sound reverberate through her. She moved one questing hand lower, and Max quivered. A feeling of pure pride shot through her that she could do this to him, that she could bring him to the same fever pitch of need that he'd brought her to.

"Caitlin," he said again.

"Tell me what you want, Maximillian." Her voice was a throaty purr.

"Make love to me, sweetheart."

"I will. Show me what to do."

Dizzy with need, Max hurriedly rolled on another condom, then guided her on top of him, groaning again when she sheathed herself around him. He was captivated by her smile—the smile of a wanton, of an angel. He would give his life to keep that smile on her face, Max thought before the fog of pleasure eclipsed everything but the driving necessity to find the ecstasy only she could give.

When Max woke up it was light, and based on the rumbling of his stomach, probably after eight.

Caitlin still slept, her head cradled on his shoulder. He smiled. So it hadn't been just one more dream. It had really happened. He tightened his arms around her and she stirred, murmured incoherent words, and pressed her face into Max's chest. Her warm breath stirred the hair there, and Max felt a sudden tightening in his body. All he had to do was think about her to want her again. He didn't think he'd ever get enough of her.

Last night had been so much more than he'd ever expected. The first time they'd made love, Caitlin's response had been shyly passionate. But the second time Max would carry engraved in his memory forever. Caitlin had been Eve, Delilah, Helen—a woman secure in her own femininity. A temptress, a siren.

There had been a third time, too, in the middle of the night, when both were warm and hazy from sleep. Caitlin had cuddled in his arms as if she belonged there. And she did. She might not know it yet, he mused as he brushed her hair from her face, but he would never let her go.

Caitlin opened her eyes to an empty bed, but she could hear the muted sounds of Max whistling in the kitchen downstairs. She smiled. Max's off-key tune was the prettiest music she'd ever heard.

She sat up, looping her arms around her knees, feeling some unfamiliar aches as she did. They were good aches, however, reminders of a remarkable night. And a remarkable man. There were some vague stirrings of disquiet as well, but she resolutely pushed them away. There would be time enough to deal with reality. But not now. Not yet. She wanted to carry this dream further.

The faint scent of food wafted up from the stairs, and her stomach growled in response. Swinging her feet to the floor, she glanced around for something to wear. The clothes that had been dropped heedlessly to the floor in last night's passion had been picked up and folded into tidy stacks on Max's dresser. Caitlin sighed and shook her head. Such neatness. She'd have to do something about that.

She reached out for her sweater, then changed her mind and grabbed Max's shirt instead. She had to roll the sleeves up several times, but it hung to mid-thigh, offering adequate cover.

Feeling shy, she paused in the kitchen doorway to watch Max as he puttered around. She was sure he would look sexier in tight jeans and a sweater than in the chino trousers and button-front shirt he wore. But he was already gorgeous. One couldn't expect perfect too.

Max's face lit up when he saw her, and he covered the distance between them in two strides. "Good morning, sweet Caitie," he said just before pulling her to him for a thorough kiss.

After she had caught her breath, she said, "Good morning to you, too, sweet Maxy."

"Sweet Maxy?"

"Sweet Caitie?"

"Well, you are sweet." He smiled down into her eyes, noticing how the gold flecks sparkled and shined. "I was going to bring you breakfast in bed. But since you're here, why don't you sit down and let me serve you?" He pulled out a chair and offered it with a flourish of his hand.

With all the grace and dignity of royalty, Caitlin took the proffered seat, arranging the shirttail daintily around her thighs. Did she realize, Max wondered, just how provocative she looked wearing his shirt? It was like a brand—a brand that marked her irrevocably as his.

He set two plates on the table—one with fried eggs, sausage links, and buttered toast, and one without the sausage—and two large glasses of orange juice and joined Caitlin at the table. "Dig in," he said just before biting into his toast.

Caitlin picked up her fork and sliced off a tiny bit of egg. She hadn't had a real one in years, but she figured she could manage. After all, there wasn't enough cholesterol in it to kill her. As soon as she tasted it, however, she knew she couldn't eat it.

Max had polished off his toast and half of his sausage before he noticed that Caitlin hadn't touched her food. He laid down his fork. "Is something wrong?" he asked in concern.

"Um, no, well, not really. Max, what did you fry the eggs in?"

"A frying pan."

"I know that, but you didn't use the grease from the sausage, did you?"

"Yeah. Oh." Max paused as realization hit him. "I'm sorry, Caitie. I'll fix you something else. Cereal? More toast?"

Caitlin had already seen the boxes of cereal on the kitchen counter. Not one contained less than sixty percent sugar. She picked up a piece of toast, but immediately put it down when she saw the melted butter on it.

"It's okay, Max. Really. I'll just have juice." She raised her glass and took a sip, then put that down too. It was that frozen reconsituted stuff with sugar and corn syrup and artificial flavors added. "I'm not that hungry in the mornings," she said.

"Okay." Max eyed her sharply, then leaned back in his chair. "So what's really the matter?"

Caitlin winced. Fixing her breakfast was such a nice gesture. How could she tell him she couldn't abide any of it. Not to mention that she was worried about what a lifetime of this diet would do to his health. "It's nothing, really. I'm just not very hungry." She could see from the look on his face that he wasn't buying it.

"C'mon, Caitlin. Just give it to me straight. Are you regretting last night? I didn't rush you into it, did I? I tried to be—"

"No! Oh, no, Max. Of course you didn't. Last night was wonderful."

"Wonderful, was it?" Max said, a satisfied purr in his voice.

"Don't let it go to your head."

"I wouldn't dream of it. You'd never let me get away with feeling too proud of myself." He grinned, then sobered. "If that's not it, then what is?"

"Max, I really hate to mention anything, but do you know what the cholesterol content of this breakfast is? You've got gobs of butter on the toast, eggs which are already high in cholesterol fried in sausage grease which only compounds the damage. And this orange juice isn't even real orange juice at all. It's mostly water with artificial flavors and colors added."

"Caitlin, I can understand you not wanting to eat meat, but you can't let this health stuff get in the way of a normal diet."

"Normal diet? Max, the normal diet for people thousands of years ago was mostly nuts, berries, roots, and leaves. That's mankind's natural diet."

"Yeah, well, thousands of years ago the average life-span was about thirty years too."

"That was because of disease or infection due to injuries."

"Cait, obviously that natural diet didn't keep them any healthier."

She stifled a frustrated sigh. "So you think caffeine, cholesterol, artificial colors, flavors, and preservatives are going to keep you healthier?"

"Maybe not, but I don't think eating them is like eating poison, like you do."

"Max, you aren't even trying to understand. Our bodies are—"

"If you hand me that malarkey about our bodies being temples—"

"I wasn't going to—"

"Because I don't want to hear it. You worry about what you eat and—"

"I can't help worrying about you because—"

"I'll worry about what I eat. And don't—" Max stopped. "Say that again."

"Say what again? You haven't allowed me to finish a single statement for the last five minutes."

"You said you worry about me."

"So?" she said almost defiantly.

"I worry about you too, Caitie." He paused, his eyes searching her face. "I love you."

"You love me?" Caitlin stared at him for a long moment, stunned.

"Yeah, you stubborn, hardheaded, exasperating woman. I'm head over heels in love with you."

Whatever reaction Max had expected, it was not Caitlin standing abruptly, knocking over her chair in her haste. Her back stiff, she said, "It's not necessary to say that just because we—just because of what happened last night."

Max looked affronted. "I don't say anything I don't mean."

"Max, last night was wonderful, but I'm not looking for any kind of a long-term—"

"I don't recall having asked you for one."

Caitlin fell silent. She looked at him for a long while, then turned away.

"What are you afraid of this time, Caitie?"

"I'm not afraid," she denied automatically.

"Aren't you?"

"No!" she exclaimed again.

"Oh, yes. But don't worry, sweetheart. I'm not going anywhere this time."

Looking anywhere but at the eyes that seemed to see right through her, Caitlin admitted, "Max, I need some time."

"Oh, Caitie." He gave a gentle smile. "If I gave you time, you'd use it to decide how to shut me out. I won't let you do that. I won't push you, sweetheart, but I won't go away either."

Caitlin met his gaze then and said, "I need to go pick up Jordie from Donna's."

"Fine. I'll see you tonight."

"Max—"

"Seven o'clock."

"Max—"

"I'll bring dinner. No meat. At least not for you," he said cheerfully. "Now, go get dressed and I'll run you by my office so you can pick up your car."

Completely confused by how she'd been outmaneuvered, Caitlin did as told. Whatever she said to him didn't seem to matter, she grumbled to herself. He just ignored it.

How could they have a serious relationship right now? She had too many things to deal with. There was Jordan—he was her first responsibility—and the greenhouse. Besides, she and Max were too different. He was so neat and organized and precise, while she was none of those things. She didn't want to be any of those things, not if it meant living in a house where there wasn't even one tiny piece of lint that showed a real person lived there.

And the way he ate, pumping himself full of caffeine, refined sugar, cholesterol, and all sorts of artificial things. And stubborn? She'd never met a man more stubborn than Max. He didn't even listen to her. There was just no way any kind of relationship between them could last.

When Caitlin spoke all this aloud to Donna later that morning, her friend pursed her lips, then said slowly, "Just who are you trying to convince? Me or yourself?"

Ten

That night Max arrived at Caitlin's forty-five minutes early. When no one responded to his tap on the screen door, he let himself in. The television was tuned to some cartoon and Jordan was sprawled on the sofa, sound asleep. He set the bags of food he carried in the kitchen and looked around for Caitlin. The sound of water running in the downstairs bathroom made Max head in that direction. He had his hand on the knob, when Caitlin opened it from the other side.

Caitlin saw Max, retreated a step, and squeaked, "You're early!"

"Not early enough," he said, trailing a finger along the top edge of the towel wrapped around her. "If I'd been here only a few minutes earlier, I might have found you in the shower."

"Where's Jordie?" Caitlin asked, clutching the towel.

"Snoring on the living room sofa."

"Why don't you go wake him up? If he sleeps too long, he won't want to go to bed at his regular time."

Max's eyes ran hungrily over every inch of her exposed skin, and when his gaze rested on her breasts, Caitlin felt her nipples harden in response. Max reached out and unerringly put one finger on a tight bud. Caitlin's breath caught in her throat. "Max."

Max took a step closer to her and locked the bathroom door behind him. His eyes gleamed as he said softly, "After last night, Caitie, I should have gotten at least a hello kiss."

A blush started at the tops of her breasts and spread up her neck to her cheeks. "About last night," she began primly.

"Yes, let's talk about last night, sweet Cait." His voice was as rough as sandpaper, yet as silky as velvet. "It was the most incredible night I've ever had in my life. The way your lips felt beneath mine, the way your breasts filled my hands, the way your body turned to fire around me. Only instead of feeding the hunger inside me, it made it grow to where I want you more now than I did before. Is that what you want to say about last night, Cait?"

Caitlin couldn't think of anything to say at all. His words had called up all the vivid images she had tried to hold at bay all day. And with the growing awareness, Caitlin felt a warm dampness gather between her thighs.

Her desire must have shown, because Max lowered his head to hers, stealing one kiss, then another. He sipped and savored her mouth until she responded by parting her lips. Then he crushed her in a kiss that drank greedily of her sweetness. She arched her body against his, and Max reached down and, cupping her bottom, lifted her. Her legs wrapped around him until she fit against him—her moist softness against his straining hardness.

Max's fingers slid under the terry cloth to find her bare skin and Caitlin, moaning wordlessly, shifted slightly, trying to bring that hard pressure where she needed it. Max gave an answering groan and stepped up to the vanity, where he sat her on the edge and pulled the towel away, dropping it to the floor.

He bent his head and took one nipple into his mouth, stroking it to turgid awareness with his tongue, then gave the same loving attention to the other. The tightness in his loins became excruciating. A shudder ran through his body and he suddenly buried his face between her breasts. "God, Caitie, we've got to stop. Otherwise, I'm going to make love to you right here, and I don't have anything with me to protect you."

Caitlin felt as if she were burning and only Max could put out the flames. "Max, the timing. It's probably all right." The murmured words were filled with longing.

Max ached for her so desperately, he felt sweat break out on his forehead, but he shook his head. "No, sweetheart. I'll never take a chance on that with you."

"But it hurts," she whispered.

Max smiled. "That's a hurt I can take care of." With one hand, he caressed the dewy folds of flesh between her legs. When she arched against his seeking fingers, he closed his mouth around her nipple.

"Oh, Max," she breathed, her hands fastening in his thick hair. "I need . . . I need . . ."

Max increased the rhythm of his stroking and, moments later, was gratified to feel the spasms that shuddered through her body. He pulled her into his arms and held her tightly. He felt her pleasure as keenly as if it were his own, and he was shaken to his very soul with the intensity of it. Caitlin didn't want to hear him say he loved her, so he would simply have to show her every chance he got.

Before either of them could say anything, there was a knock on the door and a plaintive "Mom?"

Caitlin took a deep breath. "Yes, Jordie?" She was gratified to find her voice sounded fairly steady.

"Mom, is Max in there?"

"Um . . ." She paused, wondering how to answer. "Why do you ask, honey?"

"Cause his car's here and I can't find him anywhere."

Caitlin cast a quick glance at Max, who pointed upstairs. "Have you checked upstairs?"

"No."

"Well, maybe he's there looking for you. Why don't you go see?"

Caitlin and Max listened to footsteps that stamped away, then Max kissed her, a quick, gentle kiss, and left, closing the bathroom door quietly behind him. One minute later Caitlin heard Jordan's shout of welcome, followed by the muffled sound of delighted chatter.

She turned to get her clothes from the vanity and caught a glimpse of herself in the mirror. She paused to stare at a sight of herself she'd never seen before. Her cheeks were flushed with fulfilled pleasure, her lips red from Max's kisses, her breasts still swollen from his touch. But the biggest difference was in her eyes. The shadows banished, her eyes sparkled with delight.

She looked like a woman who had been thoroughly loved. Hoping Jordie didn't notice and question the change in her, she quickly tugged on jeans and a T-shirt.

When she entered the kitchen a few minutes later, Max was taking carry-out cartons from the microwave. He turned to her, and his eyes held hers. Wild violets? Blue hyacinths? Bachelor buttons? There just had to be a name for the blue of his eyes, Caitlin thought.

He smiled as he said, "I don't understand it. Somehow the food got cold, so I had to heat them up."

Feeling suddenly shy, Caitlin lowered her gaze.

"*Voilà!*" Max announced, setting the cartons on the table. "Chinese. And I got vegetable stir-fry with tofu for you."

Pleasure coursed through her at his thoughtfulness. Not that she could eat the dish, since it probably had loads of MSG. But that was her fault. She hadn't told him about her allergy.

He really was the most wonderful man she'd ever met. Also bullheaded and exasperating, but wonderful nevertheless. Maybe, just maybe, whatever was between them could work out after all.

Caitlin and Max saw each other every day the following week. One night they took Jordan skating, the next Max came to her house for dinner. A couple of evenings the three of them piled on Max's sofa and watched TV. Max even took Jordan with him and his three nephews to see a movie. The thought of Max in an elegant suit sitting through a film about ninja turtles while surrounded by screaming, excited children filled Caitlin with tender amusement.

By Friday Max was ready to eat nails. He'd had a week of close contact, affectionate touching, but no satisfaction. He wanted so desperately to be alone with Caitlin, he was willing to resort to almost anything. Even bribery.

He dropped by the greenhouse in the middle of the day with flowers and lunch from the health food store she liked. He even went so far as to eat some of the spiced lentils over rice. And that was a real sacrifice, he thought. But when he asked Caitlin to come to his house by herself that evening, she demurred.

"Caitie, I want to be with you." Max walked around the desk to stand in front of her.

"You could come by my house for dinner tonight with me and Jordan."

Max sighed and tugged her to her feet, his eyes gleaming. "Caitie, the things I want to do with you are not appropriate for young eyes. I leave tomorrow for Atlanta for three days. I need to be with you before I go."

Caitlin felt a little breathless at that and her resolve weakened. "Max, I just don't think—"

Max slid his palms slowly up her arms to her shoulders, then urged her closer. "Ah, sweet Cait. I've needed you desperately all week," he said, his voice a husky rasp.

Caitlin tried to gather her rapidly scattering thoughts, but couldn't. His fingers were doing a marvelous dance up and down her spine. "Max—"

"Please, Caitie," he entreated her softly as he ran his hands up underneath the bottom of her T-shirt and splayed them over her back.

"Max—" Caitlin's eyes fluttered closed.

"Please, Caitie." His hands moved to her front and he teased her breasts over the lace of her bra.

"Max—"

He urged her into the cradle of his thighs and pressed her into his growing hardness. "Please, Caitie."

"I—ah—I'll call Donna."

"I'll pick you up at six-thirty," Max said in satisfaction.

"I'm meeting with a new vendor at six for a few minutes," Caitlin murmured, trailing her fingers up and down his chest. "I'll come straight to your house afterward. I'll even bring supper with me."

Max agreed immediately. With the touch of Caitlin's hands on his chest, he would have agreed to anything—even Tofu Surprise.

"Hi," Caitlin greeted Max when he opened his front door to her that evening. She lifted the paper bag she held in one hand. "Here's supper."

At Max's skeptical look she grinned. "Vegetarian subs on whole wheat. Hey, what're you doing?" she exclaimed as Max took the bag from her and strode into the kitchen.

Caitlin heard the refrigerator door open and shut, then Max came back into the room, walking slowly to her, one hand loosening his tie, which he dropped carelessly to the floor. His belt quickly followed. Caitlin's breath came in short, quick pants. "I guess you're not hungry right now, huh?"

"Not for food." He reached out and pulled the bottom of her T-shirt loose from her jeans waistband.

"What are you hungry for?" Even as she asked

it, his fingers flew to work the buttons of his shirt free.

Max answered the question by sweeping Caitlin up into his arms and heading straight to his bedroom. He put her down next to the bed and shrugged off his shirt in one easy movement.

Things were moving so fast, Caitlin thought. They always seemed to move fast with Max, barely leaving her time to catch her breath. "Max," she gasped, "Wait. Don't you think we—"

"No." Max unsnapped her jeans.

"You don't even know what I was going to ask."

"I know you talk too much," he mumbled, lifting her onto her toes and pressing an eager kiss on her lips. His tongue demanded and received entrance, and swept into her mouth in a series of erotic thrusts. When her body turned warm and pliant in his hands, he tugged the T-shirt over her head and undid her lacy bra.

Suddenly it seemed as if he weren't moving fast enough, and Caitlin arched her back, pressing her bare breasts against his chest.

Max shuddered as he held her more fully against him. He ached for her, burned for her. "I need you now, sweet Cait. Now." He took off his trousers, then her jeans, leaving her clad only in bikini panties. His ravenous eyes feasted briefly on the creamy white flesh before he smoothed the lace down her legs.

He fell with her onto the bed, his mouth finding hers with a voracious hunger. His hands seemed to be everywhere at once, and Caitlin gave herself over completely to the passion he evoked. She cried out when his seeking fingers found her most sensitive point, and he moved to capture that cry with his mouth.

He entered her swiftly, and they both moaned as their bodies strained together. Max's last coherent thought as he found triumphant release was *Mine. She's mine.*

Afterward Max cuddled a passion-spent Caitlin in his arms, and dreamed of spending every night with her like this. He closed his eyes and saw him and Caitlin tucking a sleepy-eyed Jordan into bed, kissing the boy good night, and gently shutting the door. Hand in hand they'd go straight to their own bedroom and make sweet love all night long.

"Max? Your dog just climbed into bed with us."

"He's used to sleeping with me." Max settled her more securely against his shoulder.

"Oh." Caitlin smiled to herself. So Max let his dog on the furniture. Maybe there was hope for him yet.

"When Charlemagne comes home with you, does he sleep with you?"

"Sometimes." Caitlin's eyes fluttered closed.

Max yawned and rested his cheek against her hair. "Well, when we get married, your cat and my dog'll just have to sleep elsewhere."

Caitlin lay beside him, her body stiff against his while she stared unseeing at the ceiling. Her old adversary, Panic, showed its ugly face again and taunted her. Get married, it sneered, so you can become weak and powerless all over again. Trust someone other than yourself and see what happens. After all, look what happened with Brad. And with your father.

As soon as she heard Max's slow, even breaths and knew he was asleep, she eased herself out of his arms. She hurriedly dressed and tiptoed downstairs.

She drove home, hearing Max's words over and

over again. *When we get married . . . When we get married . . . When we get married.* When she arrived home, she collapsed on the sofa, her knees unable to hold her up any longer. Her hands trembled.

She'd thought it was just the sex she was afraid of, but now she knew it went much deeper than that. An affair was one thing, but marriage? The very idea terrified her. Could she actually put not only her heart but her future into someone else's hands?

No! Never again. Never again would she depend on another person, another man, for anything. She was strong and independent. She would rely on no one but herself, she told herself, ignoring the soft yearning inside to run back to Max's arms, Max's bed.

Max smiled and nuzzled his face into the soft hair that tickled his nose. He planned on waking up like this every morning for the rest of his life. He reached out to pull her closer, but his hands encountered more hair. A lot more hair. Max's eyes flew open and he sat straight up in bed. Cholly raised his head up to look at him, gave a disgruntled sigh, and settled back down on the pillow.

"Caitlin?" Max looked around the room. Her clothes were gone. Maybe she was in the kitchen. He tugged on his pants and went down to check. She wasn't there either. He looked out front for her car. It was gone.

Max frowned and glanced at his watch. She probably went home to shower and change for work. He wished she'd awakened him first. If he hurried, he might have just enough time to call her from the airport before his plane took off.

When the phone rang, Caitlin knew who it was. She let it peal a half dozen times before she finally answered it. "Hello?"

"Hi, sweetheart. I was beginning to think you'd left early for work."

"I'm ready to leave now," she said.

"I missed you this morning," Max said huskily. "I'd looked forward to waking up with you in my arms."

"I needed to get home."

"I know. But I'd have loved another chance to hold you and kiss you before I left. I wish I didn't have to go."

"I hope you have a nice trip," Caitlin said politely.

Max frowned. She seemed distant this morning. "I'll call you tonight."

"That's not necessary."

He couldn't escape the niggling feeling that something was wrong. "Yes, it is. I'll miss you, Cait."

"You'll probably be too busy to miss me," she said lightly. "Well, I have to go. I have several orders to get together first thing."

"Caitlin—" Damn! He heard the last call for his flight. "I have to go. I'll call you."

"Don't—" But he'd already hung up.

When the phone rang that evening, Caitlin just looked at it. She wrapped her arms around herself and willed the bell to stop. It rang a dozen times before it fell silent.

An hour later it rang again. When it eventually

stopped, she took the receiver off the hook. She needed to hear his voice so much, but that very need frightened her. She didn't want to need anyone. It had taken seven years for her to learn to be strong, and every time Max came near, he threatened that strength with the feelings of vulnerability he brought out in her.

"Mom?" A sleepy-eyed Jordan peered at her from the bottom of the stair. "I thought I heard the phone keep ringing."

"It's okay, honey. Go on, get back in bed, okay?" Caitlin smiled reassuringly at Jordan as he headed toward his bedroom, then her gaze returned to the telephone. Why did everything have to be so complicated? she thought wearily.

She went upstairs and sat on Jordan's bed for a long time, watching him sleep. It was comforting to know that he, at least, was undisturbed by worries. She finally went back downstairs to check and recheck the locks on every door and window, even though she knew the danger lay, not in the world outside, but in the tauntings of that old nemesis that even now wouldn't leave her alone.

It was closer to dawn than midnight when she finally slept, a fitful sleep troubled by dark, shadowy dreams.

She awoke a couple of hours later, feeling as if she'd had no rest at all. She did look better than she felt, though, she acknowledged as she eyed her reflection in the mirror after she'd dressed in clean jeans and a T-shirt. She went into the living room and had barely replaced the receiver when the telephone rang. Before she realized what she was doing, her hand had already lifted the receiver.

"Where were you last night?"

"Hello, Max," she said evenly. "I'm sorry. Did you call last night?" The warm languidness that she always felt upon hearing his voice began to weaken her, but she determinedly stiffened her resolve.

"Are you all right?" Max demanded.

"I'm just fine. I'm running a little late though. Thanks for calling. I hope your trip is going well."

"Caitie, what the hell is going on? You're talking to me as if we were just introduced at a party."

It was so very good to hear his voice, she thought, even if it was currently laced with frustration. But she needed time. She needed room. He was crowding her, and it was stirring up all the old panicky feelings inside. He wanted more than she could give. He wanted it all.

"Everything's fine, Max," she said quietly. "But I do need to get ready for work. I'll talk to you later." She hung up the phone, and just to be sure Max didn't call back, she left the receiver off again.

She brought up her hands to rub her aching temples. It was going to be a horrible day, she thought. Barely seven o'clock and she already had the beginnings of a blistering headache. Maybe it was just as well, a small voice inside her said. At least it camouflaged the heartache.

When she went into Jordan's room to wake him up, he was sitting up in bed and scratching some suspicious-looking red bumps on his arm.

He looked up and frowned. "Mom, I have a headache and I itch."

Caitlin laid a hand on his forehead. It felt a little warm. And the rash looked awfully familiar. "You know what, kiddo? I think you've got what Jerry had."

"Chicken pops?"

Caitlin smiled. "Chicken pox, yes. Why don't you get dressed? I'll see if Dr. Hardy can take a look at you."

"Will it mean a shot?"

"No, sweetheart." As Jordan jumped out of bed with a muffled whoop, Caitlin felt a sudden pang. She wished with all her heart that there was a shot that could make her feel better. But she knew nothing could ease the pain inside.

After a visit to the doctor, who gave Caitlin a tube of cream to take care of Jordan's itching, she decided it wouldn't hurt to take her son to work with her and let him play quietly in the office.

When they got there, she found the red light blinking on the answering machine. It didn't surprise her at all to hear Max's voice after she pushed the play button. "Caitlin, where are you? Is everything all right? The operator said your home phone is out of order. It's eleven o'clock and you're not at the greenhouse. I thought you usually worked nine to one on Saturdays. I'll call back in an hour."

A pause followed, then another message. "It's eleven forty-five. Why aren't you at work? Your home phone is still out of order. I'm going to call back at one, and if you're still not here, I'm sending the police over to check things out."

The phone rang at twelve-thirty. Caitlin steeled herself as she picked it up. "Love, Incorporated."

"Caitlin!" Max bellowed. "Where the hell have you been?"

"Hello, Max. I ran Jordan by the doctor this morning."

"Doctor? Is he all right? I'll catch the first plane back—"

"It's just chicken pox, Max. He's fine."

"What's the matter with your home phone? It's out of order. All I've gotten are busy signals."

"I'll check it out," Caitlin murmured. "I hope your trip is going well."

"I miss you like hell, sweetheart."

I miss you too, she thought to herself, but didn't say the words out loud. "Thanks for calling, Max. I, uh, I have some things to do here before I can get Jordan back home. I'm sure you're busy too."

"Not too busy to talk to you." Max sounded worried. "What's the matter, Caitie? Is something else wrong? You don't sound like yourself."

"I'm just tired, Max. Everything is fine."

"Dammit, Caitlin! Why are you speaking so formally to me. For God's sake, don't push me away again."

Caitlin's eyes filled with tears, but she kept her anguish from showing in her voice. "I have to go, Max."

"I'll call you tonight. Your phone better be fixed by then." Max's words were clipped. "We have to talk."

"Yes," Caitlin said miserably. "I guess we do."

The safe haven of Max's embrace beckoned like a lighthouse beacon in a dense fog. She wanted to be in the harbor of his arms and never venture out to the seas alone again. But she resolutely pushed the thought away. She couldn't lean on anyone. Not ever again.

When the telephone rang that night, Caitlin let Jordan answer it. She listened as he happily told Max about his "chicken pops" and about getting to miss school next week. When Jordan handed the phone to Caitlin, her knuckles clenched white on the receiver and she took several deep, steadying breaths before lifting it to her ear.

"Hello, Max."

"How are you, Caitie?" Max's voice sounded subdued.

"I'm okay. How's your business?"

"It's going well. I should be able to leave tomorrow afternoon." Max chose his words prudently as he tried to pick his way through the mine field she'd thrown in front of him. He felt as if everything might blow up at any moment.

Why, in God's name, couldn't she tell him what was wrong? He'd told her he'd fight all the dragons she had, but he couldn't fight what he couldn't see. "Talk to me, Caitie," he urged softly.

"I just need some time, Max. Everything's moving too fast. I need some time and space."

"What are you saying?"

Caitlin made sure her voice would sound cool and steady before she spoke. "I'm saying that perhaps . . . we shouldn't see each other for a while."

"Not see each other?" Max asked cautiously. What was going on here? His heart began to pound in slow, painful thuds. "For how long?"

"I don't know."

"Caitie, I—look, we can't discuss something like this over the telephone. I'll be back by three tomorrow afternoon. I'll come straight to your house."

"I don't think that's such a good idea—"

"I'll be by tomorrow afternoon." His tone left no room for argument. "You'd better be at home."

Caitlin didn't sleep much that night either, arguing with herself as she lay in what she admitted was a very lonely bed. She loved being with Max. She loved making love with Max. But she didn't want to have to depend on him—or anybody—for anything. She couldn't risk everything on just one roll of the dice. Why couldn't they just continue their affair? It didn't *have* to end in marriage, did it?

They could go on as they were doing now, spending pleasant evenings together, making love passionately. She wasn't totally comfortable with this plan, but she was happy to come up with any kind of solution at all that would let her keep Max in her life without having to put it all on the line.

When Max arrived late Sunday afternoon, Caitlin greeted him with a smile and a kiss. If he'd been the sort of person to drop his jaw in astonishment, he would have tripped over his chin. But instead he eyed her with wariness.

"How's Jordan?" was the first thing he asked.

"He's not feeling too bad, but he gets tired easily. He's taking a nap right now." She hooked her hand through his arm and led him to the sofa. "Tell me about your trip."

"Caitlin," Max began, "we need to talk. Last night—"

"I'm sorry about what I said last night. Can we just forget it?"

"No. No, we can't. Caitie, what's going on?"

"Everything's fine now. I did some thinking last night, that's all, and everything's okay."

Max relaxed a little. She seemed to be completely satisfied and happy. He had to understand, though, what had made her try to pull away. "Caitie, I'd really like to know what's been on your mind the past couple of days. Obviously you've worked it all out, but I believe we need to be straight with each other about what we're feeling."

She fidgeted. He's right, she thought, but she hated trying to discuss it. "I just felt, well, I felt crowded. I felt like maybe I was being pushed into a long-term commitment."

"And you don't want that," Max said carefully, his face blank, his tone neutral.

"That's right. But last night I realized that we can go on being—um—"

"Lovers?" Max supplied.

"Yeah."

"Suppose I don't want that?" He sounded brittle. "Suppose I want you not only in my bed, but in my life for good, Caitie?"

"Max, I don't want a commitment right now. I'm not ready for it. But I'd still like to be with you."

Max got to his feet. "I see. I'm good enough to go to bed with, but not good enough to share the rest of your life with?"

Caitlin stood too. "Max, that's not what I mean."

"Isn't it? It's just one more way you're pushing me away."

"No, I'm not—"

Max looked bitterly weary. "Caitlin, I'm in love with a warm, beautiful woman. I want to make a life with her. And her son, whom I love as much as if he were my own. But she keeps pushing me away. I keep coming back for more, but now I'm tired. Now I feel like I'm just spinning my wheels, going nowhere except maybe backward."

He looked at her for several moments. "I'm thirty-four years old, Caitlin, and I want a home and a family with a woman who loves me as much as I love her. Do you know you've never even said those words to me?"

"Max—" Caitlin stopped. She didn't know what to tell him. "Max . . ."

"Don't say anything, Caitlin. Just think about it. If you decide you're ready for a real relationship, let me know." He sighed heavily. "But right now I'm tired, Caitlin. When it was just the past intruding, well, that I could deal with. But now it's you. And I can't fight you." With that Max left, quietly pulling the door shut behind him.

Eleven

It had been a week since Caitlin had seen Max. She'd stopped telling herself it was better this way. She no longer believed it anyhow.

At first, when she hadn't been able to sleep, feeling restless and unsettled, she'd tried to convince herself she was just too wound up. It wasn't that she missed Max. When sleep did come, it came with dreams of Max holding her, kissing her, touching her. The dreams were so vivid she could feel Max's strong arms around her, see the golden glints in his thick brown hair and his blue, blue eyes. Were they Caribbean blue, royal blue, periwinkle? She could hear the rough timbre of his laughter, and it made her want to laugh back, made her feel safe and warm. It was a laugh she could listen to for the rest of her life.

When she awoke, her whole body would ache with loneliness and she would turn to burrow into Max's embrace, but he was never there. She would then spend the rest of the day in a foul mood, snapping at everyone and muttering impatiently at work. Even Martha had come to wear a look of relief on her face when it was time to close up the greenhouse.

Caitlin had thought all along that a relationship between her and Max was impossible. He was so conservative, so neat, such a junk-food addict. He'd drive her crazy, and in no time have Jordan going to school in pinstripe suits and eating cheeseburgers. He was also stubborn and opinionated, the kind of man who would keep her from being strong, independent.

But as time passed, she found she couldn't eat and her sour disposition never improved. Each day seemed longer and lonelier and more pointless than the one before. The only thing that got better was Jordan's chicken pox, not that it made him easier to get along with. Instead, he became more cranky and grumbled why Max didn't come by anymore, especially after each of the two times Max called to check up on him.

No, things were definitely not any better now that Max was out of their lives, Caitlin thought as she sat at her desk in the office. She was staring out the small window, wistfully watching the finches fight over the thistle seeds she'd just put out.

Her mind didn't register the birds though. Instead, she saw Max—the way his hair tousled despite his efforts to keep it groomed, the gentle smile on his face when he spoke to Jordan, that little glint in his eye when he teased her. She'd give anything to see that glint now.

Her thoughts were so vivid that she could have sworn she smelled Max—that spicy fragrance that seemed uniquely him. And then she realized it *was* him. She spun around.

Was it her imagination or did he look thinner? Were those dark circles beneath his eyes? Still, despite all that, he looked good. Better than good. Wonderful. Even in his conservative dark suit and maroon tie. "Max . . ."

He gave a reserved nod. "Caitlin."

"How are you?" Brilliant, she thought. What sparkling conversation.

"Fine. I understand from Jordan that he's better." His tone of voice was polite but stiff.

"Much. He's back at school today and is even going camping with Rick and Patrick this weekend."

"That's nice," he said. He pulled a folder out of his briefcase. "Here's a copy of the contract you signed."

Caitlin wanted to cry. The easy camaraderie was gone. Not even a smile broke the bleak formality of his expression.

"Max," Caitlin called out as he turned to go.

He turned back and stood, waiting, as she fumbled for words. She wasn't sure what she wanted to say. She knew only that she couldn't let him walk away just yet. "Your nephews, um, did they get chicken pox from Jordie?"

"No, they seem to be fine."

"I'm sure your sister wasn't happy at the prospect though."

"She wasn't particularly upset. Said she'd rather have them get it over with now as opposed to later."

"Oh, well, that's good."

"If you'll excuse me," Max said, looking pointedly at his watch, "I have another appointment to get to."

"Oh. Of course. Um, thank you for dropping this by." She stood to walk him to the door.

"I'll see myself out." Max turned and left, his footsteps crunching on the gravel. They sounded more steady than he felt, he thought. Once in his car, he let out the breath he'd been holding, and his shoulders slumped in defeat. He'd hoped, he'd prayed, but apparently she still didn't want him.

His fingers clenched the steering wheel and his eyes burned. Oh, God, wasn't there some way he could make her love him? But someone either loved you or she didn't. And she didn't. That ate at him like acid. Before long there'd be nothing left inside, he thought. He'd be just a shell. He felt as if he were leaving his heart behind as he drove away.

Caitlin stared at the door long after he'd left. She felt something on her cheek and reached up to brush it away, surprised to find it was a tear. It was followed by another, then another. Soon her face was wet and her shoulders shook with her sobs. She felt so empty inside, as if she'd never be full again.

"Hey, what's wrong?"

Caitlin jumped and turned around to find Donna looking at her in concern. She hastily wiped the tears away. "Nothing. I'm fine."

"Bananas! Don't hand me that. You were crying your heart out."

"It's nothing, I told you."

"It's Max, isn't it?"

To Caitlin's dismay, she felt more tears well up in her eyes. She nodded in resignation. "I guess it is."

"So what'd you do this time?"

"Me?"

"I've known you since kindergarten, Caitlin. Even before Brad, you played it cool and distant—afraid of getting involved. Afterward, it was only worse. It stands to reason that you've tried to scare Max off."

"I think I've succeeded." Caitlin's voice was muffled. "He brought some papers by this afternoon and he was so formal, so cold." She propped her elbows on the desk and leaned her forehead on her hands. "Oh, Donna. I've really made a mess of it this time, and I didn't mean to. I was just trying to be strong."

"Strong? What're you talking about?"

Caitlin sighed. "I've been leaning on other people so long now—you and Rick, Dr. Atlee, Martha—that I felt I should take care of things myself, not lean on anybody else. And Max—"

"I think I see," Donna interrupted. "Caitlin, being strong doesn't always mean dealing with everything by yourself. It also means realizing when you need someone and not being afraid to ask for help—or for love. But for what it's worth, I doubt you've lost Max. If he loved you last week, he loves you this week. Love doesn't die that fast or that easily."

"Thanks." Caitlin sat up, already feeling better. "I still don't know what to do though."

Donna grinned. "Hey, being strong also means going after what you want. So, go get him, tiger."

Caitlin smiled back and reached for the phone. "I think I'll do just that." As Donna waved good-bye, Caitlin punched in the number to Max's office. Unfortunately, all she got was the answering machine. Sighing, she left her name and number and hung up. Just to be sure, she also called his house and left a message on that answering machine as well.

He hadn't returned her calls by closing time, so she picked Jordan up from the sitter's. When they got home she called Max's number again and left another message. But he still didn't call. "He probably doesn't ever want to talk to me again," she muttered morosely, then brightened. Maybe his appointment had just run long.

When Max hadn't called by the next morning, however, her spirits were dampened. Nevertheless, she called Martha and told her to go ahead and open up, that she'd be in later. She hopped in her car after seeing Jordan off to school and drove to the nearest shopping mall.

The first thing she did was go to the lingerie shop and look for something sexy. She'd settled on a black lace teddy, when a gold satin nightgown caught her eye. It was rather demure, but it had a mutlticolored dragon embroidered on the front. With a pang she remembered Max and his declaration about fighting her dragons the night they'd first made love. Without another thought she hung the black lace teddy back on the rack.

The second stop Caitlin made was at a men's casual wear store. She found a pair of stonewashed denims in Max's size—or maybe in the next smaller size.

By the time she arrived at work, it was nearly eleven. She'd expected Max to have returned her call by then, but he hadn't. She didn't know whether to be hurt, angry, or worried. It depended on whether he hadn't called because he didn't want to talk to her, or because he was tied up with someone more interesting, or because he'd had an accident and was lying in a hospital somewhere.

Hesitantly, Caitlin placed another call to his office, not sure if she wanted to know the truth or not. Patsy recognized Caitlin's voice right away. "Oh, hi, Caitlin. I'm sorry, but Max didn't come in today."

"His appointment," Caitlin began. "Did he get held up out of town or something?"

"No, nothing like that. He's home sick today."

"Sick?"

Patsy hesitated a moment. "Oh, yes. Really sick. Why, I even took him to the doctor this morning, and he never goes to the doctor, you know. So I knew he was feeling pretty horrible."

"Oh, dear!" Caitlin exclaimed, her heart sinking. "Is it serious?"

"You *do* care."

"Of course I care!"

"Well, Max wasn't sure." Patsy paused, then lowered her voice dramatically. "As for your question, I think he'd better be the one to discuss his condition with you."

"His condition?" Caitlin's voice squeaked.

"Mmm. Yes. Well, the other line's ringing. Gotta go. Bye," Patsy said, then hung up.

Caitlin's heart pounded and her hands shook as she placed a call to Donna. If she'd ever had any doubts about her feelings for Max, this had dispelled them. "Donna? Can you pick Jordan up from school today and keep him tonight? I just found out Max is terribly ill and— Oh, thank you so much. I'll call you later."

She picked up her purse and dashed out of the office to the front door of the greenhouse, calling to Martha over her shoulder. "Martha, I've got to go. It's an emergency. Can you close up?"

"Of course. It's not Jordan, is it?"

"No, no, it's not Jordan, but I'm not sure I'll be in tomorrow either."

She didn't get a speeding ticket on the way to Max's house, but she did get a warning. The rest of the way she barely managed to keep from driving over the limit.

Max's house looked deserted. The morning paper still lay in the middle of the sidewalk and the shades were all drawn. Caitlin sat in her car for a long while trying to gather her courage. All this talk about being strong and independent and she couldn't rustle up enough courage to go up and knock on his door.

The thought that Max simply might not want to see her made her stomach hurt. However, when she thought about Max alone and dealing with the effects of some devastating illness, her courage returned. With a decisive nod she grabbed her purse, marched up the sidewalk, and tapped smartly on the door. It opened almost immediately.

"Patsy, I don't—" Max stopped short. "Caitlin."

"What're you doing out of bed? Should you be up? Did the doctor say you could get up?" Caitlin's eyes roamed hungrily over Max's dear, familiar features. Funny, he didn't look sick.

"The doctor didn't say I had to stay in bed. Although I would have had to get up to answer the door anyway."

"Oh. You don't have to stay in bed? Do you have a fever? Did he put you on medication?" As she fired the questions at him, she took Max by the arm and walked into the living room with him. She frowned. "Maybe you'd better sit down."

"Why?"

"Max, I talked with Patsy."

"Yeah. So?"

"She told me how sick you were."

Well, bless her heart, Max thought. Maybe he wouldn't fire his meddling sister after all. When he saw the frantic, tender concern written all over Caitlin's face, the ice around his heart began to thaw. Now to make her realize that what she felt for him was every bit as real as the love he felt for her.

"I suddenly feel like I need to lie down," he said weakly.

"Can you make it upstairs?"

"If you help me." Max draped an arm over her shoulder, leaning heavily on her as she walked with him upstairs. Guilt stabbed him at the worried look on her face. But he wasn't lying about the weakness. His legs *were* shaky at the feel of her body next to his. Besides, he was fighting for his life here. For whatever reason, Caitlin had come to him, and if it was sneaky to fool her this way, then so be it.

As they went into his bedroom, images besieged him—Caitlin in his room, in his bed. Even though he'd lived there for over a year, it seemed as if all his memories of this room came from just the past couple of weeks. When he closed his eyes, he saw Caitlin, her face flushed with shyness, her warm brown eyes glowing with passion, her lips curved in a siren's smile.

God help me, he thought as hot tendrils of desire coiled in his body. It would take all his self-control to keep from laying her down on the bed and making new memories. He managed not to grab her, but his heart raced and his hands shook with the effort.

"Heavens," Caitlin exclaimed softly, "you're trembling!" She pulled down the bedspread and blanket. "Here. You'd better lie down."

Max sat on the edge of the bed and willed himself not to pull her down on top of him. To keep his hands occupied, he began to unfasten his shirt, though his fingers fumbled clumsily with the buttons.

"Let me," Caitlin urged, her hands moving to the front of his shirt.

Max stifled a groan, feeling his self-control slipping out of his grasp. "I'll finish it," he said, his voice a strained croak. He unfastened the last two buttons and pulled off the shirt.

Caitlin's eyes flew to his bare chest. She longed to throw herself on it and cling to him for all she was worth. Her gaze lingered, touching on the cords of muscle, the golden tan, the pink rash. "What?" One hand reached out to brush over it. She knew that rash.

Her eyes threw accusations at Max. "Chicken pox?" At least he had the decency to blush, she thought as red color suffused his skin.

"Caitlin, I can explain—"

"Here I am, worried sick, and all you have is chicken pox? And you even dragged your sister in on this."

"I didn't. I didn't know she would tell you I was deathly ill or anything. But when you came over, looking so worried, it felt so good, I played along with it." His voice trailed off. "I'm sorry."

"You should be, you skunk." Caitlin turned and walked out of the room.

"Caitlin, wait!" He leapt to his feet and raced down the stairs after her. He saw her head to the front door. "God, Catie, please don't go. I'm sorry. I—"

She spun around and pursed her lips. "Maximillian Tobias Shore, sit down and shut up." She pointed a finger at the sofa. Max obeyed, completely taken by surprise. Then his heart sank when she turned back to the door and left.

He heard her car door open and shut. Boy, he'd really blown it this time. She'd never forgive him. He braced himself, waiting for the hum of the engine that would take her away. He closed his eyes and dropped his head in his hands.

The front door opened and Max looked up with a jerk. A blur of heavy blue fabric hit him in the face. "Wha—" Max brushed the material aside. "Caitlin? I thought you'd gone."

"You're not getting rid of me that easily, you rat."

"I'm not?" He could feel a silly grin spread over his face.

"And wipe that silly grin off your face!" He tried to pull the corners of his mouth down, but couldn't. She could stand there and yell at him all day if she wanted, even all week. Hell, she could yell at him the rest of her life.

"You owe me for this, Max Shore."

"Anything, sweetheart. Anything at all."

"Good. Since you offered, put on those jeans."

"What jeans?" He couldn't look away from the sparkle in her eyes.

"The ones in your lap, you sneak."

"Oh, those." His eyes narrowed as he looked down at them. "I don't usually wear jeans."

"No time like the present to start, is there? After

all," Caitlin added smugly, "you said you owe me."

"Will this make you happy?"

"Ecstatic."

"Okay, then." Max stood and moved his hands to his belt buckle, his eyes watching Caitlin for her reaction. To his delight, she sat down in the chair, leaning back and crossing her legs, a smile curving her lips. If she was going to watch, he'd give her a show worth watching. His movements became slow and seductive as he slipped his belt free of the loops.

He walked over to her and dropped the belt in her lap, then picked up her hands and moved them to the button at the waistband of his trousers. "Unfasten it," he commanded huskily, and she did. He stepped away and slowly slid the zipper down, an inch at a time as Caitlin's tongue slipped out to moisten her lips.

Turning his back to her, he deliberately lowered his trousers just a little, then a little more, finally pulling them down completely and stepping out of them. He turned back, his eyes going straight to her. She had leaned forward in the chair, her chin propped on her hands and a dreamy smile on her face.

Clad in nothing but his white briefs, he picked up the denims. He then went to Caitlin's chair, perched on the arm, and pulled the jeans up over his legs. Standing, he turned back to her. "Fasten these," he said, his eyes liquid with desire.

"Later," she murmured back, standing up next to him, her eyes soft and warm. She reached out a hand and ran it over his chest, tangling in the soft brown curls. Her fingers brushed lightly over the rash. "Does it itch?"

"Oh, yes," he breathed. "And aches unbearably." He wasn't talking about chicken pox.

"Well, you mustn't scratch." Her voice was a husky whisper and a fingertip lightly stroked over his taut nipple.

He drew in his breath. "Oh, Caitie, I can't think of anything else but."

"Gee." Her fingers plucked at the other nipple. "I'll just have to think of some way to distract you." She dropped a hand then, brushing it over the bulge outlined so clearly by the unzipped jeans.

"Oh, yes," he groaned. "Distract me, Caitie. For heaven's sake, distract me."

"Maybe this will help." With one lithe movement she grasped the bottom of her green T-shirt, pulled it over her head, and rubbed the soft cotton over his chest. "Did that distract you?"

His eyes sparked fire as he looked at her. "It helps," he said huskily. "Distract me some more."

She reached around and unhooked her lacy bra, drawing it down her arms and baring her breasts to his avid, hungry gaze. "Is this distracting enough?"

"Almost." His hands lovingly encircled her breasts, his thumbs moving to stroke the rosy tips to diamond hardness.

"Well, then," she said, a catch in her breath. She took his hands from her breasts and moved them to the front of her cutoff jeans. "Unfasten these."

When he did, she slid them off. "How about now? Are you distracted now?"

"Oh, God, I'm so distracted, it's killing me. And I want you so much, I'm on fire with it."

"Then take me by the hand, sweet Max, and lead me to bed."

They never made it to bed, only as far as the sofa.

Sometime later Caitlin raised her head up from Max's chest and smiled at him, a smile so sunny, he felt as if he couldn't breathe. He had to keep that smile for the rest of his life. "So, sweetheart, are you going to make an honest man out of me, or what?"

"Guess I'll have to," she said. "I certainly couldn't let a sneaky little devil like you loose on an unsuspecting public."

His arms tightened around her and his heart filled with so much love, he didn't know if he could hold it all. "Say it, Caitie. Please, say it."

"I love you, Max. Will you marry me?"

"You bet. Hey, where're you going?" he said as Caitlin scrambled off the sofa.

"Just hold your horses a minute," she said, presenting an enticing view as she bent to rummage in the shopping bag she'd set by the door. She pulled out the satin gown and put it on. "What do you think?"

Max's gaze roamed over the slinky satin, seeing the embroidered dragon curling around her breasts. "I can see I need to fight a few dragons. Now, come here, woman." He held out his hand, his eyes glowing.

Why hadn't she seen it before? Caitlin asked herself as she slipped her hand in his. A clear summer sky. His eyes were the blue of a clear summer sky.

THE EDITOR'S CORNER

If there were a theme for next month's LOVESWEPTs, it might be "Pennies from Heaven," because in all six books something unexpected and wonderful seems to drop from above right into the lives of our heroes and heroines.

First, in **MELTDOWN,** LOVESWEPT #558, by new author Ruth Owen, a project that could mean a promotion at work falls into Chris Sheffield's lap. He'll work with Melanie Rollins on fine-tuning her superintelligent computer, Einstein, and together they'll reap the rewards. It's supposed to be strictly business between the handsome rogue and the brainy inventor, but then white-hot desire strikes like lightning. Don't miss this heartwarming story—and the humorous jive-talking, TV-shopping computer—from one of our New Faces of '92.

Troubles and thrills crash in on the heroine's vacation in Linda Cajio's **THE RELUCTANT PRINCE,** LOVESWEPT #559. A coup breaks out in the tiny country Emily Cooper is visiting, then she's kidnapped by a prince! Alex Kiros, who looks like any woman's dream of Prince Charming, has to get out of the country, and the only way is with Emily posing as his wife—a masquerade that has passionate results. Treat yourself to this wildly exciting, very touching romance from Linda.

Lynne Marie Bryant returns to LOVESWEPT with **SINGULAR ATTRACTION,** #560. And it's definitely singular how dashing fly-boy Devlin King swoops down from the skies, barely missing Kristi Bjornson's plane as he lands on an Alaskan lake. Worse, Kristi learns that Dev's family owns King Oil, the company she opposes in her work to save tundra swans. Rest assured, though, that Dev finds a way to mend their differences and claim her heart. This is pure romance set amid the wilderness beauty of the North. Welcome back, Lynne!

In **THE LAST WHITE KNIGHT** by Tami Hoag, LOVESWEPT #561, controversy descends on Horizon House, a halfway home for troubled girls. And like a golden-haired Sir Galahad, Senator Erik Gunther charges to the rescue, defending counselor Lynn Shaw's cause with compassion. Erik is the soul mate she's been looking for, but wouldn't a woman with her past tarnish his shining armor? Sexy and sensitive, **THE LAST WHITE KNIGHT** is one more superb love story from Tami.

The title of Glenna McReynolds's new LOVESWEPT, **A PIECE OF HEAVEN,** #562, gives you a clue as to how it fits into our theme. Tired of the rodeo circuit, Travis Cayou returns to the family ranch and thinks a piece of heaven must have fallen to earth when he sees the gorgeous new manager. Callie Michaels is exactly the kind of woman the six-feet-plus cowboy wants, but she's as skittish as a filly. Still, Travis knows just how to woo his shy love. . . . Glenna never fails to delight, and this vibrantly told story shows why.

Last, but never the least, is Doris Parmett with **FIERY ANGEL,** LOVESWEPT #563. When parachutist Roxy Harris tumbles out of the sky and into Dennis Jorden's arms, he knows that Fate has sent the lady just for him. But Roxy insists she has no time to tangle with temptation. Getting her to trade a lifetime of caution for reckless abandon in Dennis's arms means being persistent . . . and charming her socks off. **FIERY ANGEL** showcases Doris's delicious sense of humor and magic touch with the heart.

On sale this month from FANFARE are three fabulous novels and one exciting collection of short stories. Once again, *New York Times* bestselling author Amanda Quick returns to Regency England with **RAVISHED.** Sweeping from a cozy seaside village to the glittering ballrooms of fashionable London, this enthralling tale of a thoroughly mismatched couple poised to discover the rapture of love is Amanda Quick at her finest.

Three beloved romance authors combine their talents in **SOUTHERN NIGHTS,** an anthology of three original novellas that present the many faces of unexpected love. Here are *Summer Lightning* by Sandra Chastain, *Summer Heat* by Helen Mittermeyer, and *Summer Stranger* by Patricia Potter—stories that will make you shiver with the timeless passion of **SOUTHERN NIGHTS.**

In **THE PRINCESS** by Celia Brayfield, there is talk of what will be the wedding of the twentieth century. The groom is His Royal Highness, Prince Richard, wayward son of the House of Windsor. But who will be his bride? From Buckingham Palace to chilly Balmoral, **THE PRINCESS** is a fascinating look into the inner workings of British nobility.

The bestselling author of three highly praised novels, Ann Hood has fashioned an absorbing contemporary tale with **SOMETHING BLUE.** Rich in humor and wisdom, it tells the unforgettable story of three women navigating through the perils of romance, work, and friendship.

Also from Helen Mittermeyer is **THE PRINCESS OF THE VEIL,** on sale this month in the Doubleday hardcover edition. With this breathtakingly romantic tale of a Viking princess and a notorious Scottish chief, Helen makes an outstanding debut in historical romance.

Happy reading!

With warmest wishes,

Nita Taublib

Nita Taublib
Associate Publisher
LOVESWEPT and FANFARE